C H A T

-- A Vic

Frank Watson

Editor's Note: The following story is purely a work of fiction. The darkly fantastic world of the Chateau Noir is completely imaginary and bares no relationship whatsoever to our own reality. Whether dream or nightmare, it is but a shadow.

CHATEAU NOIR

FORWARD - AN HISTORICAL NOTE

When I first came to the Chateau Noir it was in the role of special emissary from my uncle, Lord S., a long-time contributor of funds to that special school for wayward young ladies and secret training institution for possibly the finest courtesans the world has ever known. Although I certainly had no reason to suspect it at the time, my first visit to that well-isolated estate was to be for me the beginning of a life-long fascination. There are those today who no doubt suspect the existence of places like the Chateau Noir, and there may very well be some similar institution operating even now on some other secluded country estate somewhere in the wide world. But if such a place does in fact exist, I am unaware of it.

Like many another disillusioned older person finding himself uncomfortably stranded in these lamentably "modern" times, and who spends his declining years lamenting the imagined or actual glories of the past, I believe that among the many other

precious treasures lost the privately trained courtesan must be counted.

Someone compelled to observe the competitive struggle, in the world of business and in private life that is the current state of affairs between the men and women of today could, I fear, scarcely hope to comprehend the simple beauty of a young woman strictly trained from early youth exclusively for the pleasure of a man. And that is the reason, I suppose, that drives me to pen this account of my own personal experience of those fair and distant days at that dark chateau.

Something truly wonderful in the world was lost with the death of Mademoiselle Marie T., and the subsequent closing forever of the Chateau Noir, the most singular and most secretly revered institution which she managed for nearly twenty years, all told.

I do not at all intend what I am about to set down be an historical account of the Chateau Noir. The exact location of the isolated country estate upon which the school was founded and the various biographical facts regarding the persons who made up the school's remarkable staff are, I believe, unimportant to my story, and at the time I write there are many of those who

were intimately involved with the school who yet remain among the living, although, with very few exceptions, their exact whereabouts are unknown to me. There are, at least, relatives of those involved alive certainly, and I have no wish to complicate their innocent existences by officially connecting them with what will undoubtedly be seen by some as most shameful and, perhaps, even criminal events.

All of the names and most of the places mentioned herein will therefore be entirely fictitious. The events themselves, you may be assured, are true; they were personally observed by myself, and the memories of those days are visions that will haunt me, unfaded and unblurred, until the day of my death, a day that I am informed by my physicians will not be long in coming.

The few brief background facts regarding the Chateau Noir which I will relate are simply as follows.

My uncle, the fore-mentioned Lord S., had enjoyed a career of some distinction in the Her Majesty's foreign service, and had, in consequence of that career, some frequent dealings with some of the darker Arab nations. During the course of those dealings he had had the opportunity to observe first-

hand certain singular, ancient and time-honoured methods used by the men of that region in training their young women for service, both within the most unique Arab version of the institution of marriage and without, a system which involved the carefully balanced application of the strictest, indeed sometimes most cruel forms of corporal discipline, combined with the exaction of the most intense and utterly pure experiences of sexual pleasure the female of the human species has ever known. Those who are familiar with relationships between the sexes as they existed in England during the reign of our late Queen Victoria will readily understand the startlingly attractive contrasts such an exotic and altogether foreign structure of sexual relationship presented to a man of my uncle's repressed and, I believe, wholly unnatural era in British society.

To put it simply, a Great and Singular Idea at length was formed, and with the help of certain other men of great means, acquaintances who shared a similar fascination for the more exotic Arab way of life, my uncle, upon returning to the West, founded on the Continent what was to become the world's finest school for the

training of what the French call courtesans, though the splendidly unique product of this particular school would expand and fulfill the meaning of that word in such a way as would put any courtesan in service before that time to humble shame.

The Chateau Noir enjoyed many years of successful and profitable life before the school was dismantled due to an impending investigation by the French government. As governments become ever stronger, life in the main becomes ever duller.

There are those who maintain that there is something to be learned from any history. The task before me here is but to simply and as accurately as possible relate the events encompassing my experience with the Chateau Noir exactly as I saw and felt them. The interpretation of those events, what they might mean for society, indeed, what they may might mean for all of Mankind, what these events have to teach the World, I leave for the reader to decide for himself.

T.S.

CHAPTER ONE - ARRIVAL

Nothing my uncle had said to me previous to my departure for that distant part of the continent could have prepared me for my first experience of the strange and beautiful Chateau Noir. Really, I had been told very little; simply that, as I was now a young man of eighteen years of age, it was high time I had some practical experience of the world. And for that reason, it was my uncle's intention to send me on an errand of business to the continent.

I was told by my uncle that I would be staying for some few weeks at the residence of a "very dear friend" of his, a friend who held the most respected position of Head Mistress at a special finishing school of some sort or other that my uncle helped to support.

I was also told, somewhat suspiciously I thought, that the exact location of the place to which I was to be sent was forever to be held in the strictest of secrecy.

From this I secretly assumed that I was in actuality to be the guest of one of my uncle's immensely wealthy acquaintances on the continent, perhaps at some highly exclusive pleasure resort, and that the story regarding the "business errand" was simply a bit of fiction to allay any suspicion on the part of my parents.

My uncle's considerable reputation for sometimes associating with some of the rougher elements of what is called "low" society, as well as with the higher echelons of "decent" society, was well known to me through various hints and allegations overheard throughout my childhood. The ruse of the "finishing school" had no doubt been designed to deceive my mother as to the true nature of my journey; she had never wholly approved of my uncle, and had agreed to my coming under his influence, even for so brief a time as a few short weeks, only after the strongest warnings and protests.

And so, with all these delightful and intriguing suspicions in mind, I prepared myself for some weeks of extended parties, revels of all-night dancing and delicious sport among the pleasure fields of luxury

among my uncle's forbidden "acquaintances", and nothing more.

When I took leave of my uncle at Victoria Station, I carried upon my person from him a letter of introduction addressed to one "Mademoiselle Marie T.", but the most important cargo I carried was another series of letters addressed to the same lady, some from my uncle and, as I was to learn later, others from many of the richest and most powerful men in Europe.

I also carried among my luggage a small wooden case, locked and bound in iron, it's interior most heavy with gold. I was told that this considerably weighty amount of money was to be a charitable donation to what I was again given to believe was an exclusive finishing school for young girls. The money, according to my uncle, was to assist this great and laudable institution in the many and various works of charity with which it was frequently connected. I, of course, assumed the money was in fact intended as an advance payment to my uncle's "acquaintance" for the expenses that would be incurred during my luxurious holiday; the exquisite food, the exotic entertainment would, no doubt, cost a small fortune.

When I arrived at the Chateau itself, after many long days of travel by train and boat and ornate private coach, and a surprisingly long ride along an extensive stretch of private road, which rolled through the hills for some miles even after we had passed through the main gate of the estate, I soon came to realize that this "school" was something much more larger than I had expected.

I shall always remember huge great pile of stone and wood, silhouetted against a fiery summer sunset, as the carriage approached along the cobblestone drive to the rear of the great building, a rambling three story complex, surrounded by high hedges, which also enclosed one of the most beautiful and well tended gardens I have ever seen. There was a coach house, and many other outbuildings on the estate as well. Overall, the Chateau Noir gave the impression of a pleasant combination of absolute beauty and total isolation.

Mademoiselle T. met me as I descended from the coach and approached the Chateau's carved oaken doors. She was a tall woman, dark, with a certain, slight, indefinable touch of the exotic about her calm, thin mouth and quiet, watchful eyes. I

felt myself thoroughly examined, as a great physician might examine a patient, that physician knowing instantly and instinctively all there is to know about the patient, his many quirks and ailments, both physical and spiritual, and having no need whatsoever for questions or answers. It was not the sort of look one expects in a woman, and I have never known a woman to look at me that way since.

Wordless and respectful servants took my bags, all except the one containing the portfolio of letters and the small wooden case of gold, which I attended to myself, and I was conducted by the Mistress alone down a long candlelit hallway and into an ornately beautiful drawing room.

This drawing room was richly decorated, the walls of dark paneled wood covered with fine, dark tapestries with traces here and there of fine gold embroidery that glittered in the light from many thick and exotically scented candles mounted in gold and silver candlesticks, which were scattered here and there throughout the room. Deep, rich oriental carpets covered the stone floor. A fire crackled in the large fireplace, beside which there stood a brass and iron rack containing the usual poker, cinder shovel

and hearth brush. The same rack also contained some curiously fashioned instruments that I was at the time at a loss to identify, among them were what appeared to be a variety of pokers that ended in round, rather than pointed, tips.

Mademoiselle T. and I made ourselves comfortable on plush velvet chairs and, after glancing for some moments through the pack of letters I had presented to her, my father's letter of introduction included, and having sent the heavy case of gold away with a servant, who had entered the room in response to a bell that rang somewhere far within the depths of the house at a single, gentle pull of one of the many-coloured bell ropes that hung along the wall near where she sat, the Mistress began at last my education as to the real nature and purpose of the Chateau Noir.

"You appear to be a fine young man, Thomas S.," Mlle. T. said with a tight smile. "I do not know your mother, but I knew your father very well indeed."

Marie T. was a singularly beautiful woman. Her age would have been hard to guess precisely; perhaps thirty, perhaps thirty-five. She wore a simple dress of the day. She wore her dark hair high upon her

head, tightly, but not severely. No, the detail of her aspect that suggested severity was the cold darkness of her eyes, and the somewhat cruel line of her mouth. Even when she smiled there seemed to be a message of warning. She appeared proper, finely mannered, and perfectly controlled. Her entire aspect sent the message that this was a woman of great and singular Will.

"Did your father tell you much about my school?" she asked.

I told her that I really knew very little, other than that the school was a very private and very exclusive sort of finishing school for young ladies. Frightfully expensive, I would imagine.

The Mistress smiled. "The Chateau Noir is indeed a finishing school for young ladies. Wayward girls, mostly. And it is, as you say, frightfully expensive. We have nearly twenty students attending at this time." The Mistress's smile widened slightly. "Would you like to meet some of them?"

I replied, politely, that I would be delighted, if to do so would not interrupt the young ladies' studies.

"Oh, no," said Mlle. T., with a tight smile. "In fact, Thomas, I try consider meeting the few, rare visitors we receive

here at the Chateau to be an integral part of the education of my young ladies." So saying, the Mistress put her hand to the group of coloured bell ropes, selected the blue one on this occasion, and pulled it sharply six times.

After a very few moments, there was a cautious tapping at the drawing room door and, at the Mistress T.'s bidding, there entered six timid young girls, aged approximately fourteen to eighteen years, who quickly arranged themselves in a straight line, shoulder to soft shoulder, across the centre of the room, facing Mlle. T. and myself.

They were all six dressed alike, but in no girls' school uniform the like of which I had ever seen before. They each wore instead a short, brief tunic of some gossamer fabric, silk perhaps, beneath which it could be readily determined that there were no undergarments of any kind whatever covering their variously sized young breasts. And since the hem of these tunics extended not far below the girls' waists, the small white panties the girls wore beneath were almost completely exposed.

I stood silently astonished.

Mlle. T. smiled at my reaction. "The Chateau Noir is the world's foremost training school for courtesans, Thomas. Your father and I began the school five years ago, and we have procured and trained over a hundred girls since then."

The Mistress walked slowly up and down before the line of girls as she spoke. "My girls are carefully instructed in the ancient ways of pleasure gathered from cultures from all points of the globe. Cultures easily as ancient as that of Old Egypt." She stopped and stood for a moment, facing a red-haired girl of about sixteen. "Did you know, Thomas," the Mistress said, continuing to speak to me, even as she stared directly into the bright, nervous eyes of the girl before her. "Did you know that in ancient Egypt there was a cult which explored the sexual pleasures that could be derived from the bite of the common adder?"

"Snakes?" I murmured in response.

"Oh, yes," the Mistress whispered, into the face of the red-haired girl. "You see, they observed that the convulsions preceding death due to snake bite closely resembled the tremors of the deepest climax of sexual pleasure. So they fed snake venom, in ever

increasing volume, to certain young slave girls, until eventually they were rendered immune to the poison, but not to the intense convulsions following a bite."

The Mistress gazed even more intently into the eyes of the now trembling girl before her. "Girls who had been rendered so immune were brought into the temple of the serpent god on special days. They were tied down spread-eagle on a stone altar and jars filled with poisonous adders were pressed over their young breasts."

The red-haired girl before her gasped, suddenly, earning her a quick look of contempt from the Mistress in response.

"Then," Mistress T. continued, "while they held the first two jars in place, the priests would press another jar of serpents between the girl's legs."

A slight whimper came from one of the other girls in line, perhaps from the youngest, a small-breasted brown-haired girl of fourteen.

Mlle. T. did not seem to notice the interruption. "It is said that the girl slaves would appear to orgasm for hours at a time after being submitted to the Worship of the Snake, being repeatedly bitten and bitten and bitten again. Most died, due to a lack of

educated supervision on the part of the priests. But do you know what, Thomas?"

I did not respond. And the girl before Mlle. T. stood tremblingly silent as well.

"I have perfected those techniques!" the Mistress said with a cold smile. "The serpent-induced orgasm can continue for days without undue damage to the individual. I have even determined that for some reason, as yet unknown to me, red-haired girls seem to have the ability to endure the most!"

A look of inexpressible horror swept over the red-haired girl's face as she heard this, a look which Mistress T. seemed to drink in with great relish.

"Carl!" Mistress T. called, suddenly. Almost instantly, there was one of the servants I had seen earlier, standing behind the red-haired girl, with a firm grip upon each of her elbows.

The girl struggled with a fierce effort, but was helpless in the servant's iron grip.

Mlle. T. then turned away from the girl, to face me, and continued her speech, most casually. "This is Karen, Thomas," she said, indicating the red-haired beauty. "Karen has been consuming a most special diet since her arrival here, some two months ago. You see,

there is very little taste to distilled snake venom, as Karl, here, prepares it." This was apparently the name of the tall, dark servant who held Karen up before us. "Just one of our Karl's many talents; he is also a Master Chef, you know. Well, Thomas, our Karen here has been practically immune to serpent venom for nearly a week now. And as soon as our shipment of live adders arrives this week, Karen is going to experience pleasures that no woman has known in over two thousand years!" Mlle. T. laughed, coldly.

The girl, upon hearing this, issued forth with the most piercing scream I had ever heard, and she then fainted dead away in the servant's arms. At Mistress T.'s bidding, the servant hoisted the unconscious girl over his shoulder and carried her from the room.

"I'm afraid our Karen will have to be watched very carefully until her little playmates arrive," Mistress T. said, laughingly. "Our last red-haired girl hanged herself with her own bed sheets when she heard of my intentions toward her. A shame, really. I understand the Worship of the Snake was thought of as quiet pleasurable for some of the Egyptian slave-girls. There are rumours, in fact, that the Queen of the Nile herself, the great

Cleopatra, put an adder to her own breast in envy, after observing one of her slave girls endure a ceremonial snake-induced orgasm that latest for an entire month!"

I shivered, but did not know whether I did so in horror or in fascination. A quality, a sensitivity, that I did not realize I possessed had been planted within my being, and was even now beginning to grow and take root.

"This... is Stephanie," Mlle. T. said suddenly, awakening me from my brief reverie. "Isn't she lovely?"

The Mistress was now standing before another of the girls, a brown-haired nymph of about sixteen. Her breasts were smallish, but of a tautness that promised greater things to come as she grew and developed.

The woman lifted one hand to the young girl's cheek and wiped away a single tear that hung there. "Are you frightened, Stephanie?" the Mistress asked, softly.

"Y... yes, Mistress," the girl in question replied, tremblingly.

"No, Stephanie," Mlle. T. said, comfortingly, as her hand stroked the girl's pale cheek. "Why be afraid? Is there anything to be afraid of here?"

As she spoke, Mlle. T. began to slowly trace one finger down the girl's cheek to the pulsing softness of the girl's neck, from the hollow of her neck down to the softer swelling of the girl's left breast, its subtle shape clearly defined under the wispy fabric of the short tunic. Then, bringing the fingers of her other hand into play, the Mistress stood, lightly stroking the tips of both the girl's young breasts through the thin tunic.

"Thomas," Mistress T. called, softly, but insistently. "Come here."

I came, as if in a dream. I walked along the line formed by the other four girls, standing nervous, but docile, watching what was taking place, until I came to stand by young Stephanie and her Mistress.

"Stand behind her, Thomas" the Mistress said softly.

I did so.

"Now, Thomas," continued Mlle. T., in a soft, hypnotic whisper, "do you see the small catch at her shoulder?"

I saw it. A tiny, silver hook against the thin fabric, which I now identified as fine silk.

"Release it, Thomas."

I did so and the filmy white tunic slipped from Stephanie's smooth shoulders and fell

unheeded to the carpet at her feet, leaving the soft breasts bare, and the girl's entire quivering form, except for the brief, white silk panties she still wore, nakedly exposed in the shimmering firelight.

"Now, Stephanie," said Mlle. T. "Do you feel better?"

"Oh, Y... yes, Mistress," the girl whispered, a frightened look in her eyes.

"That's fine," said the Mistress. "Now, I want you to do something for me, Stephanie. Something very simple. Do you understand?"

"Yes, Mistress" she murmured. Stephanie's eyes were now closed, and her soft breathing had become heavier."

"Listen to me, Stephanie," said Mlle T. "You are not to come. Do you understand?"

The girls whimpered suddenly.

"Stephanie," the Mistress said again, this time most intensely. "You are not to come! Do you understand?"

"Pleeeeeeeeease, Mistress!" the girl cried, suddenly, imploringly.

"No, Stephanie... you are not to come! You know this game. Do you understand? Answer me!"

For some moments, the young girl seemed beyond words, so intense was her

anguish. Warm, glittering teardrops rolled down her cheeks, unheeded, as she was suddenly racked with sobs.

I could simply not understand why the girl's reaction should be so despairing. From what little knowledge I had of the female sex, this gained from the pages of certain disreputable and forbidden books obtained from one of my schoolmates, girls, on the whole, seemingly had to struggle to attain their illusive female orgasms. Why, then, was this young girl so afraid of disobeying her Mistress by succumbing to an unwanted climax?

On the other hand, I was struck with a certain admiration for Mlle. T.'s establishment of unquestioning discipline in so young a girl. Stephanie obviously had an absolute horror of disobeying her Mistress, in any matter whatsoever.

"Stephanie?" the Mistress continued. "You must answer me. Just because you lost this game the last time we played it does not mean you cannot win it this time, does it?"

More sobs, but somewhat quieting now.

"So, do you understand the rules? Do you accept?"

"Y... yes, M... Mistress," Stephanie sniveled, finally.

I saw a look of triumph in the Mistress's eye.

"Very well," said Mlle. T. "We can begin. Thomas, please remove Stephanie's panties."

"Noooooooooo, Mistress, pleeeeease," Stephanie shrieked at this.

"Stephanie!" Mistress T. yelled, suddenly, shocking the young girl into a quivering silence. "Shut up this instant! Just because you have never played the game bare doesn't mean we can't now! You are being trained to control your sexual emotions. You must control your emotions so that you can concentrate on pleasing your future partners! Do you understand?"

"Yes, M... Mistress, but..."

"There are to be no qualifications, Stephanie!" said Mlle. T., cutting through the girl's objections. "Now, tell me, Stephanie. How many love strokes from the Tongue was your punishment the last time you lost?"

"N... nine minutes worth, Mistress", the girl sobbed, miserably.

"Very well, for this game the penalty for losing will be more."

"Nooooooo, nooooooo, oh, you cannnnnnn't..." Stephanie cried, in absolute panic.

"Quiet, now, Stephanie! The penalty will not be inappropriate for a girl of your strength and age, and you have had more than enough training by now to be able to fight temptation. Stand still, Stephanie. Thomas, remove Stephanie's panties."

I stepped forward once again, uncertainly. At last, I stood so close as to feel the young girl's heat. I could readily scent her sharp perfume. It was not some expensive scent from one of the world's great perfumeries. It was, instead, the natural scent of fear, softened, I thought, by a faint but perceptible hint of feminine arousal.

Though but a girl of sixteen, it was clear enough, through the evidence of my own senses, as well as from the very nature of the "test" Madame had devised for the young woman, that of resisting giving in to orgasm, that Stephanie had a more than readily aroused appreciation for the pleasures her firm, ripe body could afford herself.

It was from this, however, still unclear to me then whether Stephanie was a stranger to physical love with men, although it was

certain that she was more than acquainted with the pleasures that another of her own tender sex could provide. It was, in fact, the purpose of Mlle. T.'s experiment to see if the girl could restrain herself from enjoying such attentions to the point of spending.

My mind filled with these rushing thoughts, I did as Mlle. T. instructed me. I approached the girl from behind, knelt, and I must confess that it was with hands that trembled nearly as much as the young girl herself that I gently drew down Stephanie's single remaining garment, my fingers brushing lightly against the damp flesh of the girl's outer thighs, my face mere inches from the soft, plump curve of her firm, young behind. Her warmly radiating flanks shivered at the sensation, and a soft fretful whimper escaped from her tightly closed mouth.

"Come, Stephanie," Madame laughed chidingly. "We have not yet even started! Do you think the Tongue so light a penalty that you would succumb so early?"

"No, Mistress!" answered the young girl, pitifully.

"Very well," said Madame. "Thomas, place your hands upon Stephanie's

shoulders. You are to steady her from behind."

I followed her instructions. A shiver ran through the girl's body as I gripped her soft shoulders lightly, but prepared myself to tighten the grasp should it be required.

Mlle. T. stood facing the girl. From where I stood, behind Stephanie, I could observe the Mistress's gaze, as she stared intently into the eyes of her young student.

"Now, then, Stephanie," said Madame. "We shall begin."

With both hands, Mlle. T. began to lightly caress the girl facing her. Her fingers lightly stroked from the girl's soft young shoulders, where I held her, down along her willowy arms to where Stephanie's hands hung trembling at her hips, then up again along those narrow hips to pause ticklingly near the girl's tender underarms. I could feel the tension in the girl's shoulders as she fought to show no reaction to her Mistress's caresses.

Madame's hands now moved inward, brushing lightly to the tips of Stephanie's pert breasts, where they paused for a moment to draw light concentric circles around the girl's pink, puckered young nipples.

"Hard as little diamonds already, are they not, Stephanie?" Mlle. T. commented, quietly.

"Y... yes, Mistress," the girl answered, her voice the tiny squeak of a frightened mouse.

I leaned slightly forward over the girl's shoulder to see that the small points did in fact look painfully hard.

"Hard as little diamonds," Madame said again, quietly. "I wonder if that most precious of jewels is equally hard, Stephanie. You know, the one you keep between your legs?"

The young girl whimpered once again at this hint of much more intimate caresses to come.

"Well, Stephanie?" Mlle T. demanded, teasingly. "Can you feel your little ruby of delight becoming firm, becoming hard for us? Does is ache, Stephanie? Does it burn?" Madame asked, with a smile.

"I... I... oh...," the girl struggled for words with which to reply.

"Answer me, Stephanie!" Madame demanded threateningly.

"It... it feels... it feels..."

"How?" Madame asked again.

"I... I... I..."

Madame appeared to have lost patience. "Is this as much as you have learned about expressing the feelings of love? Is it for this that you have received your education in the literature and poetry of love? So that now you can say nothing? I ask you again, Stephanie... the jewel between you legs, how hard does it now feel?"

"I... I..."

At this point Mlle. T. appeared to lose her control and chose a most direct way to express her anger.

"Does it feel as hard as this?" Madame cried, suddenly grasping the girl's small nipples between thumbs and forefingers and twisting them sharply in opposite directions.

The girl lifted beneath my steadying hands, still planted firmly upon her shoulders, and shrieked loud enough to deafen me for an instant. Where my inexperienced hands found the strength to hold her I shall never know, but I held on tightly, a fact which Madame seemed to notice with a mix of pride and admiration, as if pleased to note the first inkling of a possible shared nature between herself and the young man who had so recently entered her world. There was also to be read in the

fiery look within her eyes the promise of further shared adventures to come.

At last, Stephanie became quiet again. I looked once more over the girl's shoulder and found the reddened state of her tender breast tips to be as clear evidence of her pain as had been the sudden violence of her reactions.

"Since words appear to fail you, Stephanie," Mlle T. continued, "I suppose we shall have to investigate the state of that lower treasure ourselves."

With this, Mlle. T. lowered herself to her knees upon a plush purple cushion she had placed before the trembling girl. Mlle. T.'s face was now on a level with the very treasure house of which she had spoken. She looked up into Stephanie's now tearful face and began her exploration.

The woman's left hand circled behind and around the girl's left thigh in order to further steady the girl during what was to be the final stage of her test. Her right hand now slipped slowly up between the downy thighs in inevitable approach to the light brown curled delta above. Her hand paused as the fingers softly brushed the first wispy tendrils.

"Now, Stephanie," said Mlle T. "This is the test. This is the moment. You must not think of the pleasure. You must not enjoy it. You most ignore it. You must think only of the payment you must make if you fail. Think only of the Tongue. Think only of how that will feel. I promise you that you will not be able to so much as move for days afterward. Your little jewel will feel the size of a grape. It will be erect and burning both day and night with that strange combination of constant arousal and the most excruciating pain you have ever known, Stephanie. You will seek release from your arousal, but will be unable to do so because that achingly swollen little fruit will be impossible to touch. You will try to play your little private midnight games with yourself and the entire household will be awakened with the intensity of your screams the moment your soft little finger makes the slightest contact."

"No, Mistress!" Stephanie cried in horror and fear, her tears now a torrent. "No, pleeeeease!"

"It is what awaits you, Stephanie," Mlle. T. continued. "Untold pain... unless you can ignore the pleasure. Now, be brave. Be strong! We begin."

With these words I felt young Stephanie's shoulders stiffen beneath my hands, as the Mistress's fingers made their first contact with the warm flesh at the apex of the girl's thighs. Her head tossed back, lifting a cascade of chestnut softness into my face.

"Uhmph," the girl moaned as Mlle. T. began a thorough and methodical massage of the soft woman-flesh she'd found.

"She is wet," Mlle. T. commented, for my benefit. "She is very wet. I fear she will she will not stand the test this time. A pity. The Tongue is such a cruel mistress. Much more cruel than myself. I would wish nothing but love and pleasure for my little charges. But pleasure... true pleasure... comes only through discipline. A young girl, to become a true courtesan, an true artist of the flesh, must never become a slave to pleasure. Pleasure must serve her. I have known many young women capable of experiencing the exciting peak of the most intense erotic pleasure for great lengths of time, and to hold themselves at the brink of fulfillment for as many days without succumbing. The intensity of the final orgasm at the end of such a period is something that men can never know, and

few women, and then only through carefully cultivated discipline and absolute control. That is what our Stephanie is learning now. She has been deprived of pleasure since the last opportunity she had to prove herself. She has been watched throughout the day so that she has had no chance at pleasure. At night she has lain tied in her bed with her hands unable to reach that place between her legs that so pitifully begs to be soothed. The natural pressure on a healthy young girl of our Stephanie's age to masturbate is, I assure you, Thomas, something strong beyond our ability to measure. On her last night she was actually observed to experience a small, insignificant orgasm spontaneously, while still tied in her bed. It was not a release, actually, but some sort of a physical safety valve, apparently. We administered a light sedative to her after that which has prevented any future occurrences of that sort, and so the pressure has been left to increase unabated, until now."

All this time, as Mlle. T. explained all this, she continued with her skilful ministrations, while young Stephanie, the subject of the little lecture, remained standing stiff and trembling between us, I

holding firmly to her shoulders, and Mlle. T. tightly in charge of the girl's lower portion.

Now and again, as her Mistress's fingers caressed some particularly sensitive spot upon the girl's young womanhood, Stephanie would suddenly stiffen into an even greater tenseness, as she fought against her every tendency towards pleasure that nature had endowed her with.

I now noticed that by looking across the room to a into the glass of large wall-length mirror that hung there I could look full into young Stephanie's face. The girl stared, vacantly, as if into an great, infinite distance. Only now and again, as her Mistress's caresses brought forth some more intense stimulation, would a slight tick around the eyes, or a small trembling of the lip betray the violence of her private, interior struggle. Then, an instant afterward, her eyes would once again harden, and her stare would focus at some object even farther removed from this fire-lit room, and there she would find the extra measure of control she needed, and both her face and her passion would become controlled once more.

"Well," said Mlle. T., as she observed these same facial changes from below. "We may have underestimated our Stephanie.

She is really doing rather well." There was, I thought, a note of disappointment mixed with the pride in her tone. "Perhaps our Stephanie has learned what must be learned after all."

I noted a slight hint of relief pass over Stephanie's mirror-reflected face.

"Just a moment more, Stephanie, and you shall have proved your metal." said Mlle. T. "Just a moment more... and..."

Stephanie suddenly erupted beneath my hands.

"Ahhhhhhhhhhhh!" she shrieked, as I struggled with great effort to maintain my hold. I could not imagine what had happened. Then I looked down and saw that while Mlle. T. had spoken those soothing words, to the effect that Stephanie's trial was nearly at an end, she had moved the hand that had been steadying the young girl's left leg around to cup the girl's hind cheeks, and apparently, while the girl had been least prepared, she had, all in a motion, thrust one long forefinger deeply into the girl's hindmost nether opening.

Mlle. T.'s strategy was now all too plain. The unannounced intrusion into the young girl's behind had been designed to so startle the poor girl that her tenuous self control

would be at last broken, and with that would come the deluge.

The plan succeeded admirably. No sooner had Stephanie recovered from her shock and surprise than she instantly became aware of her broken concentration. I looked once again into the mirror. Stephanie's face registered both shock and surprise, and then, finally, horror and panic. Then young Stephanie made what proved to be her fatal mistake. She dropped her gaze to look down into the powerfully burning eyes of her Mistress below. She saw her Mistress smile, knowing that all was lost. She appeared to struggle once again, in a last attempt to regain her failed concentration and control, and then, with a shriek as full of hopelessness and despair as any soul bound in the tortured caverns of hell could emit, she stumbled for a second upon the crest of her release, and then gave herself over to it fully.

For a full five minutes, Stephanie screamed and convulsed in our hold, as the carefully avoided climaxes of weeks past churned through and bubbled forth from the girl's strong young body, until she collapsed with a final, wailing shriek that trailed out, long and mournfully, its dying echoes

absorbed and consumed by the thick and unsympathetic walls of the Chateau Noir.

CHAPTER TWO - INTRODUCTIONS

Once again, the manservant, Karl, was called upon, this time to remove young Stephanie from the room. She fell from our arms into his, unknowingly, for she was still in the unconscious bliss of the devastating climax that had been the result of her failed test. She would, Mlle. T. assured me, have much time in the next few days to regret her failure and to contemplate the price she must pay.

"You shall see how our Stephanie adapts to her restraints. We shall visit her this very evening," said Mlle. T. "And, of course, time permitting, you may be present at Stephanie's Tonguing when the event occurs. In any event, there will be many other opportunities for you to judge for yourself the effects that intense discomfort may have in stimulating erotic satisfaction in a girl of Stephanie's unique sensitivity."

Mlle. T. now turned to the four young girls who remained with us in the room, and who had watched the proceeding events with

curve, each subtle nuance of Beverly's ripening femininity.

"She is beautiful, is she not?" the Mistress asked softly, seemingly in actual awe at the young girl's tender loveliness.

I did not answer. It was not necessary. Nor, I must confess, would it have been possible. The sights and sounds of the Chateau Noir that I had experienced thus far had left me quite incapable of speech. I could scarcely think, much less translate my confused thoughts into the spoken word.

"Now, Beverly." Mlle. T. continued. "We must show Thomas that the rest of you is no less a vision of perfection. Your panties, now, my dear."

Beverly closed her eyes with a small whimper, hooked her thumbs beneath the waistband of the tiny garment, and quickly slid them down her slim thighs and on past her knees, where they joined the little white pile that was her previously cast off tunic. She then righted herself, and stood awkwardly under her Mistress's gaze. The girl was truly beautiful.

"There is only one thing that unfortunately contrasts and mars this girl's perfection." Mlle. T. said at this point, again demonstrating the air of professional

detachment she had shown earlier when young Stephanie was being tested. "Beverly, please assume the Cat position."

Instantly, the well-disciplined girl dropped to her knees upon the hard floor and sat in the manner of the classic Egyptian feline presented in much of the statuary of that period, her feet tucked beneath her small, bare bottom, knees pressed tightly together, hands resting palm downward upon her thighs. Her head was bent downwards in the subservient attitude of an obedient slave.

Mlle. T. stood before the girl, and motioned me forward as well.

"It is a small imperfection, it is true, but one which can be easily rectified. Knees apart, Beverly, as wide as is possible."

The girl instantly did as she was told. Her knees spread apart, with a motion that somehow touched a secret place deep within my person.

"Now, lie back, just as you have been instructed, far back."

Some degree of gymnastic training was apparent in the way young Beverly now bent her supple body backward, until her shoulders actually touched the hard floor. The tender divide of the girl's young sex was now prominently displayed before us.

we desire. Something must be done. And it will be done. Up, now, Beverly!"

The girl quickly unbent from her awkward position and stood again stiffly before her Mistress.

"Tonight, Beverly, you will report to my chamber at midnight. Do you understand?"

"Yes, Mistress," the girl replied, quietly, obviously as in the dark, as was I, at what Mlle. T. had in mind for her. Indeed, apart from a shaving, a procedure which the Mistress had already denigrated, what could be done to remedy the problem of the girl's voluptuous vulval curls?

Mlle. T. caught my look of perplexity, and winked at me slightly, with an almost mischievous smile.

"Thomas, I would like you there tonight as well." she said. "My chamber, at midnight. Then all will become clear."

Mlle. T. then proceed to introduce the remaining three girls, who stood quietly awaiting their Mistress's command. They each disrobed for our examination, as their two sisters students had done before. Each was as lovely in her own way as the others had been in theirs.

There were two girls of sixteen, Ariel and Jennifer, who appeared to be exact

opposites in temperament, if not in looks. Both were dark. Both displayed a certain timidity, but that timidity was somehow manifested differently in each. Ariel, for all that she was described by Mlle. T. as being currently virginal, gave the impression of an already awakened sensuality that was quite palpable in the confident way she stood, unconcerned over her nakedness. Jennifer, on the other hand, although reportedly the more sexually experienced of the two, seemed somehow less comfortable with her knowledge of eroticism. She had, in fact, "known" a man. But for all of that, she seemed somehow more untouched than her compatriot of the same age.

The last girl to be introduced was Allison, an overtly haughty and proud young beauty of seventeen. Her hair was cut in a saucily short pageboy style. Her shoulders she held straight and defiant under our intimate visual examination. Of all the girls, Allison alone had the courage to meet our gaze, and when my own eyes met hers, it was I who felt the challenge and looked down, feeling defeated, and even somewhat embarrassed. That a naked and vulnerable young woman could inspire such a chastened reaction in a fully clothed male

said much for the girl's spirit and power. Mlle. T. seemed to notice my reaction and, calling me aside for a moment, informed me whisperingly, while out of the girl's hearing, that just as there were ways to correct young Beverly's imperfection, there existed means just as effective for curbing the unattractively daunting hostility toward males that marred the attractiveness of this older girl. Wait, she said once again, and I would see and understand all in time.

The faithful Karl imposed his presence upon us at this point to announce that dinner was served. The girls were dismissed, stooping to gather up their wispy garments as they went, and Mlle. T. and I went in together.

There was good food and good wine, and a few hours of much needed rest to look forward to.

And midnight would come, all in due time.

CHAPTER THREE - DINNER

Dinner at the Chateau Noir was both simple and elegant. Simple in so far as the food, itself, was concerned, consisting of a brace of fine roast ducklings, with a singularly delicious savoury cream sauce, garnished with chestnuts, raisons and various other dried fruits, complimented perfectly with an excellent dark burgundy. But the presentation of the meal was a study of elegance, even disregarding the unusual "decorations" with which the dining chamber had been fitted. These delightful trappings I will describe momentary.

The ever present Karl was our only servant, and he did admirably well in that role, moving silently around the great oaken table, and never allowing the wine glass of either myself or the Mistress to run dry.

I suspected at the time that this Karl also held the position of cook at the chateau, but I later discovered the presence of another servant, a much younger man than Karl, but of apparently the same national origin. In

fact, the similarity between the complexion, features, and build of the two men led me to believe them to be actually related by blood, but the exact nature of that relationship, whether of brotherhood or, perhaps even, of father and son, I never quiet discovered. I did learn, however, that it was this other I had to thank for the exceptionally fine meals at the chateau. This other servant, answering to the name of Alex, I was also to discover possessed quite a few other specialized talents, and I would have ample opportunity to observe many of them demonstrated over the course of my stay.

As to the room in which this dinner was held, it was of a large and luxurious capacity. The massive oaken dining table, although presently set for myself and Mlle. T. alone, could easily have accommodated a party of twenty or more. Mlle. T. and myself sat facing one another across one far end of the long, polished expanse.

And here I must begin to describe the most unusual decorations that had been arranged to embellish our dining enjoyment. The light in the chamber, other than that provided by a massive stone fireplace situated near the centre of one long wall, was provided by the flames of eleven flickering

candles. Eight of these candles were held by four exquisitely naked young girls. Two of the these, in age not more than fifteen, stood on either side of me at the table, and the two others stood flanking Mlle. T. as she sat opposite. The four stood motionless with a silver candlestick held in each hand. Their stares were unflinching and entirely frozen, as if they were not even aware of our presence.

I did not recognize these girls as members of the group to whom I had been earlier introduced, and Mlle. T. informed me that these were students much farther along in their training than the newer arrivals I had met. The concentration and self possession these four young women demonstrated spoke eloquently of the effectiveness of their Mistress's training.

These four, as I have stated, accounted for eight of the eleven candles which provided the glowing light for our meal. The remaining three candles were held by an even more unique human candelabrum.

Upon the centre of the table, between Mlle. T. and myself, there lay another young girl, perhaps a year older than her sisters who stood. This girl, a beautiful blonde-haired nymph of exquisite feature and

composition, lay upon her back, in profile, between her Mistress and myself. In each small, bare hand she held a single lighted candle, the melted wax of which ran freely over her clenching fists, so that by mid-meal the fists, themselves, were all but covered with the congealing flow.

This alone would have accounted for more than a small bit of discomfort on the girl's part, but there was a further reason for the girl to regret her current situation. The girl had been forced to pull her knees so far forward that they actually rested upon the table at each side of her head.

The reason for the girl's placement in this uncomfortable position was this: the eleventh candle in the room had been inserted deep within the young girl's naked, upturned sex. The position the girl had assumed was necessary to keep the lighted candle upright. And the upright attitude of the candle was extremely desirable, it was more than apparent, because an upright candle tends to drip the less.

By carefully balancing upon her shoulders and upper spine, the girl could keep the candle somewhat erect and the hot dripping of the wax to a minimum. The laws of physics being what they are,

however, a certain amount of dripping wax was unavoidable, thus complicating the girl's situation. It was imperative that the girl remain motionless in order to minimize the flow of wax. But whenever that unavoidable minimal droplet finally came, the tracing of that searing rivulet, running either forward and down across the girl's tensing belly or, more alarmingly, coursing to the rear to trickle down between the girl's trembling nether cheeks, the reflexive bodily tremor at the intense pain resulting would only serve to shake loose even more of the hot wax to be scattered in both directions.

Throughout the meal, I watched the progress of the flame from this eleventh candle as it moved ever downward with its melting. From time to time, as the dripping wax produced the effects I have described, the girl would emit a slight whimper or, at a particularly copious precipitation of hot wax, an even sharper cry.

Mlle. T. casually informed me that the young girl was undergoing another of the Mistress's intricately designed tests of will, and I could well gather from the Mistress's frowning looks in response to the girl's restrained outbursts that the subject's performance was not considered satisfactory.

Finally, Mlle. T. called for brandy, which the faithful Karl immediately brought. The Mistress herself poured the amber liquid from its ancient, dust-covered bottle.

The candle between the legs of our "centre-piece" had by this point, our meal being now nearly at an end, burned down almost to within an inch of the soft pink lips of the girl's young sex, and I had been silently concerned that the girl might actually suffer some more acute pain, and possibly even actually disfigurement, should the Mistress's "test" continue much longer.

It was at this point, however, that Mlle. T. apparently intended to bring the test to a conclusion. She was now reaching forward across the girl's upturned and tensing young buttocks and endeavoring to warm her half filled snifter of brandy in the heat of candle flame now nearly guttering between the girl's trembling legs.

"You have done well, my dear," said Mlle. T., although her expression, as seen by me, and not by the girl to whom she spoke, demonstrated that she felt just the opposite of the approval she expressed.

The Mistress swirled the warm brandy in the glass above the candle flame, as the young girl seemed to relax somewhat at the

apparently nearing end of her extended discomfort.

"But, perhaps," purred Mlle. T., "one final test is called for."

With this, the Mistress sloshed the swirling brandy out from her glass and onto the loins of the young girl, whereupon the entire pool of sweet liquor exploded into bright blue flame which washed instantly down across the girl's belly in front and into the sweet crack of her raised buttocks behind.

The girl shrieked as loudly as I have ever heard any animal cry in anguish either before or since. She bucked and writhed mindlessly for an instant as if galvanized. Then, flinging away the candles she had held so patiently in her hands, she plunged her wax-coated digits into her now fiery, wax-covered loins in a disparate effort to extinguish the anguishing flames that curled luxuriously about between her legs.

At that moment, the servant, Karl, arrived once again upon the frantic scene, no doubt at his Mistress's earliest instructions, equipped with a large pitcher of water, icy cold from a neighboring stream, which he summarily splashed across the lower body of the screaming young girl, extinguishing the

blue alcohol flames, but causing with yet another eruption of startled cries, these at the too abrupt transition or temperatures, from fiery hot to icy cold, upon the girl's tender young flesh.

"You have failed the test, do you hear!" cried Mlle. T., with scream of her own. "Take her away!"

In a few moments, writhing and sobbing, the hysterical girl had been carried out of the room and away to some other part of the building.

Collapsing back into my chair and sipping my own brandy, in order to regain my composure, I became aware of an amazing fact. Throughout the entire melee, which had climaxed our dinner, even when our female centre-piece had been shriekingly set alight, none of the other four girls, who still remained standing by our chairs with lighted candles of their own, had ever made the slightest move, had shown not even the slightest change of expression.

No emotion.

Total control.

CHAPTER FOUR - APPROACHING MIDNIGHT

In the final hour before midnight of that first day at the Chateau Noir, I was summoned from my bed chamber by Mlle. T. herself. She held in her hand a single lighted candle in an ornate silver candlestick, which cast a misty glow over her strong features, softening them a bit, it seemed, though it could well have been an illusion. Indeed, an illusion it must have been, for I cannot say for certain that, during all the many years I have known Mlle. T., I have ever seen her demonstrate any true emotion other than what would suit her strict adherence to her philosophy of stern severity as concerning the training of her students. Severity, not for it's own sake, but as the best means for attaining a very specific end. An end which on that first night at the Chateau Noir remained a complete mystery to me, but that would later on become clear.

There was method to Mlle. T.'s cruelty. And her methods almost always attained her desired results.

"At midnight," reminded Mlle. T., "our young Beverly is due in my chamber for an exercise that I believe you will find quite interesting. But there is yet time now, I should think, for a brief tour of the sleeping arrangements we provide for our students."

"But will we not disturb their sleep by visiting them in their bed chambers at so late an hour?" I asked.

"Not all of them are asleep, I believe," she responded, with a tight, knowing smile. "And besides, we have here at the Chateau a means of observation that would not disturb the lightest sleeper among them. Come," said the Mistress, leading me out into the corridor.

Our way dimly lit by the flame of her candle, Mlle. T. led me through a virtual maze of darkened passageways, passing though a number of doors, and finally arriving at the base of a long, narrow, winding staircase. This staircase ascended to a small landing where we were confronted by a tall, narrow door, covered in what appeared to be a plush black velvet.

"This is the door to our observation corridor," Mlle. T. said, quietly, as she fitted a small iron key into the door's lock. "Because of our methods of instruction, Thomas," she continued, "it is of the utmost importance that we be able to observe our young charges at all hours, day or night, in order to assure that their training is proving effective.

"A strong-willed, stubborn young girl can very well pretend, by day, to be accepting the lessons of her training, when in fact, by night, she is a private resistor. We therefore make it a practice to see that all our girls behave in private as they are instructed to do in class. They do not know that we watch them, you see, so in their assumed privacy, they unknowingly reveal themselves for what they truly are.

"Also, there are lessons and activities we assign the girls to perform on their own, which we would have no other way of determining their accomplishment were it not for the ability to directly monitor those activities.

"Most of the girls, for instance, during some point in their training, are forbidden the private pleasures of self-love. We do this in order to teach them control of their

senses through self-control and self-denial. After many hours of direct and indirect stimulation they must lie in their beds at night with the day's accumulated passions simmering within them unquenched.

"At other times a student is ordered, after a full day of repeated stimulation and climax, to continue the activity on her own, within the assumed privacy of her own bed chamber, until she has attained a set minimum number of masturbatory orgasms before she can surrender herself unto the balm of sleep.

"All these activities are secretly monitored for completion and any failures are thoroughly punished upon the following day, although it is always a complete mystery to the girls themselves as to how their failures have been detected.

"Here, you see how it is done," Mlle. T. said, as she quietly pushed open the velvet door. It slid in with a hush of air and I soon found myself within a long, dark corridor, the ceiling and floor of which were lined with more of the same plush black velvet material that had covered the heavy door.

Along the walls of this corridor I could just make out large sections of black velvet drapery, which framed what appeared to be

windows of some sort, in height about six feet and in width about four. Something, certain vague shapes, that I assumed to be in the night-shrouded courtyard outside the building, glimmered and shifted beyond these windows. My eyes could barely make out these indistinct shapes, for my vision remained somewhat dazzled by the flame of Mlle. T.'s candle, which flickered near our faces.

But now, with a single puff of breath, Mlle. T. extinguished this candle and, very gradually, my eyes grew accustomed to the deeper darkness.

I now saw that the velvet framed rectangles of glass, which lined the corridor as far as the nebulous darkness permitted my vision to reach, were not windows giving onto the outside of the building at all, but were windows that gave view rather into the insides of a long series of bed chambers, which apparently were situated along either side of the corridor. There were no doors leading into these rooms from the corridor in which we stood, but, as one walked along within the velvet lined corridor, one could look through the series of gilt-framed windows, and easily see into each of the bed

chambers, and so observe the activities of the occupants within.

As my vision became more and more adjusted to the faint illumination that now came from out of the bed chambers themselves, the purpose of the corridor became more clear to me.

"But how can they not know that they are observed?" I whispered to my guide. "If we can see in through these windows, then surely they can see out."

"But, you see," replied Mlle. T., not at all bothering to keep her voice low, "these are not windows. They are mirrors."

"What? Mirrors?", I exclaimed, still endeavoring to keep my voice down. "But, I don't understand."

Mlle. T. smiled slightly at my confusion. "Specially constructed mirrors," she said. "If fact it was your uncle, himself, who bought them from a glass maker in Egypt and had them sent here for the very purpose of constructing this chamber. You see, these mirrors are so designed as to appear as mirrors from one side, that side facing inward to the girls' bed chambers, but to function as a clear glass window from the other side, that side on which we now stand. The inner chambers are always visible

because they are always lighted, however subtly, as we insist the girls keep at least a single candle burning in their rooms throughout the night, as a further exercise in discipline, as we tell them.

"And the unusual thickness of the glass, as well as the close velvet wrapping with which this corridor is lined, makes them impervious to the slightest sound.

"We can, however, due to a special vent which opens into each chamber through a complex series of air baffles, hear sounds from within these chambers as clearly as if we were standing within the rooms themselves. But no sound we make here can be heard by the occupants within. It is an ingenious design, is it not?"

Indeed it was. And, as we drew near to the first mirror/window that presented itself to our view on the left wall of the corridor, an even truer appreciation of the architect's gift filled me with unqualified awe.

The scene through this velvet framed window, lighted from within by the single candle Mlle. T. had predicted, showed a small bed placed lengthwise not two feet from the inner surface of the glass. There was a small night table placed at the head of the bed and almost against the glass window.

And, as the lighted candle had been placed upon this table, and so burned between the window and the bed, the figure upon that bed was as ideally illuminated for our view as if she had been lying on the lighted stage of a theatre.

I recognized the girl immediately. It was young Allison, the haughty and proud brown-haired girl of seventeen, the one who had held herself so aloof from our examination earlier in the day, and the one who's defiant spirit Mlle. T. had hinted to me would be effectively broken in time, no matter how willful and self-determined the girl appeared now.

Here again, however, the girl was displaying yet another side to her self-absorption. Where earlier she had maintained an attitude of total self-control and emotional restraint, while under the gaze of her Mistress and myself, and had suggested the attitude of a young lady for which the display of anything like uninhibited passion would be unthinkable, she was now quite obviously involved in just such an undisguised act of passion.

Allison lay upon her narrow bed, her short sleeping tunic worked up above her smooth hips, and both her hands were busily

occupied between her widely parted legs. The gleam of the candlelight upon the shiny wetness upon her inner thighs, and upon the fine sheen of perspiration that graced her intently creased brow where a few damp brown curls lay plastered, told us clearly that the girl's private passion was already nearing it's peak.

The approaching crisis was heralded as well by the regular little moaning grunts and gasping exhalations that reached us easily through the conducting baffles of the sound vents.

"See the passion of which this one is capable?" Mlle. T. said, a hint of admiration in her voice, as a proud art instructor might speak of a rough-talented new student who, despite a decided need for polish and refinement, showed the clear promise of a bright future.

"Such power!" she exclaimed. "When her spirit has at last been broken and the true extent of her passion released, our Allison will something to reckon with, I assure you," she said. "I can see great things in this one."

An sudden increase in the intensity of the young girl's self-induced sensations manifested itself at this point by a general stiffening of all her limbs. Her eyes, which

had previously been squeezed tightly shut, now flew open in an expression almost of fear at the climax that was quickly rising within her. Her back arched, and one hand reached violently out to clutch a handful of the white bed sheet beneath her, as the other fairly flew in a rapid back and forth movement against the tender summit of her young womanhood.

Then, with a sharp scream, her body erupted inward upon itself, hunching and contorting. Again and again came the arching of the back, the scream, and the subsequent writhing collapse back onto the bed.

At last the girl's exhausted hand fell away from her wet centre, though for some seconds afterward a tremor of isolated after-shock now and again radiated out from her fluttering centre to tremble the girl's strong young body from head to toe, as she gradually recovered her composure.

Allison looked somewhat dazed in the aftermath of her passion, and perhaps somewhat ashamed of her temporary loss of control. Finally, she sat up and in a thoroughly businesslike manner pulled her brief tunic back down to modestly cover herself as best she could, arranged herself

primly, and folding her hands chastely above her waist, settled herself for sleep.

"Look at her," remarked Mlle. T. Her voice now held a trace of disdain. "She regards herself as pure as the driven snow. In the morning she will no doubt deny to herself that such a thing as private passion were possible. It must have been a wicked dream, she will tell herself. Such false prudishness is very difficult to eradicate. Very difficult, indeed. She will take much work, this one," said Mlle. T. as we stepped away from this window and approached the next.

Here we saw young Stephanie once again, not many hours since her "testing" by her Mlle. T. This was the brown-haired girl of sixteen who, as I had then observed, had been unable to resist the intimate caresses of her skilful Mistress.

Stephanie's chamber as well was lighted by a single flickering candle, and by it's light I saw that she lay bound to her small bed with straps of soft leather in such a way that, as Mlle. T. explained it to me, the girl could have no manual access either to her soft breasts or to that sweet secret treasure between her legs which was her great weakness.

The girl's wrists were tied, bound together at the head of the iron bedstead, and her ankles were similarly fixed to the frame's far end. The only movement possible for Stephanie was the one she made now, a sort of writhing effort, which caused her finely muscled thighs, which she pressed close together, to abrade each other in a slow and deliberate manner.

"There are many in the world like our Stephanie," said Mlle. T., thoughtfully. "Girls who have known the pleasures of men at too young an age, when their bodies have fully developed but their minds have not. She is therefore unable to control her primitive desires and thereby, the true power of her sex. See how, even now, with the ordeal of the Tongue awaiting her, she is unable to resist the insistent demands of her body."

It was true. Even though bound in such a way as to prevent the direct stimulation of her nether intimacies by way of her own hands, it was apparent that Stephanie was seeking release by other, less direct, means. The slow, deliberate frictioning of her inner thighs was clearly having a self-pleasing effect on the girl, as she quietly struggled towards, at least, some semblance of orgasm.

As we watched, she appeared to approach the achievement of her goal with a slight gasp and trembling shudder that flowed upward through her tense frame. But all deteriorated suddenly, and she fell back from the summit of her release with a small, lamenting cry of frustration.

Stephanie's near climax had not satisfied her and, after a moment, during which her body lay limp against the coverlet, she again began the same slight shifting of her thighs as before.

"She knows she cannot obtain any real release through such indirect efforts. But see how she tries. She will be absolutely frantic by morning. The Tongue will teach her to control such impulses."

At this, I inquired as to the nature of this ordeal to which young Stephanie was to be subjected, but Mlle. T. only smiled and demanded my patience. I would see for myself, she assured me, soon enough.

The two of us then passed further along the corridor and soon stood before another of the gilt-framed windows. The chamber into which we now gazed was somewhat larger than those we had seen so far, evidently because it was intended to accommodate two of Mlle. T.'s students instead of only one.

There were two of the small iron beds, although only one of these was occupied. Two young girls lay upon this bed, their coltish limbs intertwined in a lethargic embrace, their lips pressed softly together in a tender kiss.

When the two faces separated at last, I recognized the girls as Ariel and Jennifer. Ariel - the dark, virginal, but somehow knowing young one, whose innate sensuality had been provocatively obvious in her sensuous movements and shy glances. And Jennifer - the somewhat timid, though apparently physically more experienced of the two. So much alike did these two girls appear that only through the contrasting difference between Jennifer's short-cut straight black hair and Ariel's somewhat longer mane of raven curls could the two be readily distinguished one from the other.

"The Blissful Idylls of Lesbos," murmured Mlle. T., as we gazed in upon the entwined couple. "Our Ariel has long maintained a taste for female games. This is something we encourage here at Chateau Noir, as part of every girl's training. Many of our customers wish to see the girls they purchase entertain each other in that exotic

way from time to time. However, in Ariel's case there is a slight complication.

"You see, a certain French gentleman, who's name would no doubt be familiar to you, and for that reason I will refrain from mentioning it, has already chosen young Ariel as a future acquisition, subsequent to the completion of her training, of course. This gentleman's tastes are quite specific. He wishes the girl to be totally devoted to the pleasure of men, to the exclusion of her own fulfillment by any other means. He requests that Ariel be conditioned, not only against the pleasuring of other women, but also against the solitary pleasuring of herself.

"Our reputation at Chateau Noir rests on our unfailing ability to meet out client's requests, and so our Ariel has been destined for a most unusual treatment. Rather severe, I am afraid, but one which I must admit I have always found fascinating.

"Ariel has been designated for pruning. The procedure shall take place within a few days."

This "pruning" signified nothing more to my mind than had the earlier mention of the "Tongue." But I did not direct an inquiry toward Mlle. T. I assumed that all, as she

had said before in response to my inquiries, would be made clear to me, if the Mistress so intended.

Meanwhile, the girl we had been considering removed herself smoothly from the embrace of young Jennifer, and turned head-to-tail with her companion, in order to join with her in an even more intimate embrace, covering the inner thighs of the somewhat reluctant girl with a series of precocious kisses, starting at the girl's knees, and then moving quickly upwards to areas of more vulnerable sensitivity.

With these insistent caresses, Jennifer's reluctance seemed to melt like a frost before fire, and soon she began to emit soft sounds of love, followed by increasingly urgent cries of devotion and, at last, a sudden and almost despairing wail of release, after which she collapsed into the arms of her amorous bed mate, who now comforted her tenderly through the shuddering sobs that followed the pleasure-storm's peak.

"These two will spend most of the next few nights at these amusements," said Mlle. T., "even though such games have been specifically forbidden to them both, due to the circumstances I have described. Jennifer's punishment has already been

selected. And as for Ariel, she must, I suppose, be allowed these last few nights of girl-play, for after her destined treatment, such games will be quite beyond her."

Once again, as I followed Mlle. T. further down the corridor, I found myself wondering at the nature of Ariel's "impending treatment", the "pruning", and, indeed, Stephanie's promised "session with the Tongue."

The "Tongue?" "Pruning?" What could such words mean?

It was soon after this that our my tour of the student bed chambers of the Chateau Noir came to an abrupt end, for the small gold watch that Mlle. T. carried on a chain at her waist soon began to chime softly with a musical, crystalline pinging sound.

Twelve notes. It was now midnight, and Mlle. T. and I had an appointment to keep.

CHAPTER FIVE - BEVERLY

A small fire had been lighted in Mlle. T.'s private chamber, a richly appointed, luxurious room paneled in dark wood, as were most of the apartments at the Chateau Noir. Upon one wall of this chamber stood the head of a very large bed, constructed of ornately carved mahogany, and curtained in red silk hangings, so that nothing of the mattress or the bed clothes could be discerned.

The fire had been set in a medium-sized brick fireplace in the wall opposite. And directly in front of this fire, arranged in a most intriguing position, was young Beverly, the petite nymph of fourteen who had been the third of Mlle. T.'s students to whom I had been introduced earlier in the day.

An ottoman, upholstered in padded leather, with a sort of frame attached, had been placed lengthwise before the fireplace. Into this frame Beverly had been strapped in such a way as to hold her lying nakedly upon her back with her slim legs elevated and the

junction of her thighs spread into a very wide "V".

Mlle. T. approached and spoke, quietly, to the girl.

"Are you comfortable, Beverly?" she asked.

"Y-yes, Mistress," Beverly replied timorously.

"Very good," said Mlle. T. "We want your position to be comfortable, Beverly, so that you may concentrate more fully on the sensations which you are about to experience."

Mlle. T. knelt down and spoke more softly into the girl's ear.

"Some of it will be hard, my dear, but you must be brave. Most of your sisters will know ordeals much more serious, so you must not lose courage. Remember Karen's appointment with her serpents of the Nile."

The girl shuddered, visibly, at the thought of what Karen, the red-haired student, had been promised earlier.

"You must not lose your courage. The discomfort you must now know will be only prelude to the delights that will follow soon after. Without evil, my dear, there cannot be good. Without pain, there can be no pleasure. Do you understand?"

Young Beverly looked nervously about her, sniffing back a tear. "I ... don't know, Mistress."

"You will understand in time, my dear," Mlle. T. said finally. "For now, simply, be brave."

Mlle. T. rose and crossed the room to a bell cord which hung near the chamber door. No sound was heard within the room, but a bell must have rung somewhere in the building, because in a moment there was a knock and a beautiful young woman of oriental decent quietly entered with a covered tray.

"Thomas, this is Jo Lin. She is one of our special tutors here. She is from China. Our Jo Lin was apprentice to one of the great houses of Fu Won, and was brought to me, at very great danger and expense I shouldn't wonder, by your very uncle."

The face of the oriental beauty remained composed, but there was the slightest flicking glance of interest directed towards me, perhaps in attempt to detect any resemblance between myself and the relative she had known, I gathered, so intimately. There seemed to be a slight note of warm recognition in the instant before her face returned to an expression composed

peacefulness which I was to learn was her custom.

"Jo Lin is a master of certain... therapies... that were developed by her great people thousands of years ago. She is the only expert of her kind in the world."

Jo Lin smiled, ever so slightly, and gave a barely perceptible bow of her head, in acknowledgement of a complement fully deserved.

"You may make your preparations," said Mlle. T., and the beautiful oriental, with an economy of motion inherent in the best of her race, crossed the room, and seated herself upon a small upholstered stool that had been placed between the spread-eagle Beverly and the fireplace.

Mlle. T. motioned quietly for me to follow, as we approached as well.

Jo Lin, having settled herself upon her stool, and having placed the covered tray she had carried with her upon a small table to her left, turned to examine - as did I, you may be certain - the naked "V" formed by the widely spread and upturned legs of the naked girl before her.

How can I describe the sight that the three of us beheld? Beverly, a slight, through undeniably athletic, girl, at the first

fresh bloom of her womanhood, spread openly before us, the delicate lips of her young sex presented to our view unhidden, except by its light covering of a down-like fur, this just slightly darker than the golden tresses that flowed from the girl's head.

Although Mlle. T. had described the wisps of Beverly's nether covering as something which marred her otherwise perfect beauty, I confess I could not share that opinion. Indeed, the delicate strands seemed to me quite few in number. And these few yellowish curls seemed to me a pleasant augmentation, a compliment to the girl's beauty, instead of a detraction from it.

I mentioned this thought, quietly, to Mlle. T. and, at the same time, was somewhat surprised to find myself so bold. "You must trust my judgment in this," Mlle. T. replied, noting my boldness with some pleasure. "To the client for which our Beverly is intended, it is a defect. A defect which must be corrected and shall be corrected now."

"Am I to be shaved, Mistress?" It was Beverly, herself, who spoke in a small voice that was breathless in timidity.

"No, my dear," Mlle. T. said, soothingly, and then added, "Trust me, my dear, and all will be well. Karl!"

Karl, the Germanic servant, who had been standing, arms folded, in another part of the room stepped forward. In his hand was a black cloth which I saw to be a large scarf of fine silk.

Mlle. T. took the scarf from the large man and once again knelt by the head of the young captive.

"Now, my dear, you must wear this cloth as a blindfold. Do not be afraid. It is simply a custom, a part of the ceremony," said Mlle. T., as she placed the silken blackness across the young girl's eyes. In the instant before they were covered, I saw in those sweet, wide, blue eyes a remarkable mixture of trust and apprehension, and once again noted the extraordinary effect that Mlle. T. had upon her young charges. Then the eyes were covered and the black cloth knotted tightly behind the girl's head.

As soon as Beverly's eyes were covered, there came a change in Mlle. T.'s expression. There was a coldness, a cruelty, that she must have been suppressing while under the young girl's gaze, but which now radiated in her manner and filled the room.

"Karl!" Mlle. T. spoke again to the manservant, this time a bit more sharply.

The man came forward, without a word as always, and in his hand this time was a short bar of India rubber, some six inches in length, at each end of which had been attached a small-linked silver chain.

The use to which he put the device defined it's purpose. It was a "bit", like that used on small ponies, except that this bit consisted of hard rubber instead of hard steel.

Before the young Beverly knew what was happening, if, in truth, she had the slightest idea even then, Karl had placed the bit securely between her jaws, and he had hooked the short chain at either end to small, matching eye-bolts set in the ottoman to either side of the girl's blonde head.

Now somewhat alarmed, Beverly now reacted with some degree of fright, struggling to twist her head about, in an attempt to displace the rubber intrusion. But the attachment of the small chains holding the bit in place also served to keep the girl's head in a fixed position, facing straight forward. Finding this side-to-side direction of movement was now restricted, Beverly tried for the first time to move the rest of her

body. This was equally impossible. The straps which held her hands firmly at her sides, those which secured her shoulders and upper torso to the padded ottoman, and those which secured her legs to the frame of the apparatus, all held Beverly in place, quite immovable.

For the first time now, the girl began to show elements of real panic. But she soon gained possession of herself and, with some great effort at self-restraint, became still again.

It was then that Mlle. T. nodded to Jo Lin, and the oriental beauty slipped the cover from the silver tray placed at her side. Upon this tray were an assortment of metal instruments, which the woman's delicately strong and elegantly manicured fingers moved among for a moment before selecting from their midst a small pair of tweezers.

Now I guessed the exact nature of the ordeal awaiting the trembling young girl before us.

"The plucking may begin, Jo Lin," said Mlle. T.

Beverly's partially covered face registered confusion upon hearing this word, "plucking." Then, as Jo Lin leaned close between the young girl's legs, carefully

selected a single, golden wisp with the silver tweezers, closed its jaws upon it securely, and slowly began to pull, the girl was in mystery as to her fate no longer.

With the first, gentle tug, she let out a startled gasp, followed by a sharp yelp as the pull gradually became stronger. Then there came a wild shriek as the single hair was pulled, "plucked", rooted from its socket, and Jo Lin sat back, depositing the plucked curl in a small crystal bowl, which also lay upon the silver tray at her side.

As the realization came upon the girl that this slow, excruciating process would continue on until every errant tendril had been plucked from her stinging young womanhood, she became very frantic indeed.

There was a continuous screaming, mewing and yelping now, only slightly muffled by the rubber bit between her tightly clenched teeth, as these first few curls were extracted from the sweet junction of her thighs.

As the process continued, however, Beverly seemed to somewhat reconcile herself to her discomfort, and manifested the fact by reacting to the tugs and nips of Jo Lin's tweezers with only a steady

whimpering, punctuated by an occasional sharp gasp as a particularly reluctant curl put up special resistance before succumbing.

Then, as her oriental tormentress moved in to attack those tiniest of threads, sprouting closest to the very lips of Beverly's small sex, the girl's earlier shrieks were renewed, and soon surpassed in volume those that had proceeded them.

On two occasions the process had to be stopped altogether, as Beverly's consciousness failed her and she fainted, falling limp within her bonds. She was soon revived, however, with a single whiff from a small bottle which Mlle. T. held beneath the girl's nose.

On another occasion, and this as Jo Lin had come to those final few tendrils that adjoined the girl's nether lips themselves, the girl became quite hysterical, convulsing in her bonds and thrashing against her restraints in such a manner that Mlle. T. actually seemed to fear the girl might suffer some injury. Extra restraints were brought in, attached, and the process was some resumed.

The entire ordeal lasted for over two hours.

For some moments after it was finished, I stood by the side of Mlle. T., as she examined Jo Lin's handiwork. The trembling cuntal lips of the nearly exhausted young girl were now puffed and brightly inflamed, and not one single curl remained upon the girl's nether region, from lip to mid-thigh. To be sure, it was a most arresting sight.

The girl, herself, was almost insensible by this time. Her cries had all but died out by this time, though once every so often she would give a start and a gasp as if a last forgotten hair had been plucked. Mlle. T. explained that these "ghosts" of her previous pain would return to the Beverly now and again, possibly for many weeks, but were no real cause of concern. Indeed, she assured me that the entire experience would have no harmful effect on the girl whatsoever.

"On the contrary," Mlle. T. continued, "the lasting result of what our Beverly has just undergone will be one that she will find quite pleasant. There will be an extra sensitivity in those tender regions that will manifest itself in an almost instantaneous state of animal arousal whenever that area is touched."

Mlle. T. laughed shortly. "In fact, you will find little Beverly will be very busy with herself over the next few days simply striving to keep her sweet, girlish hungers adequately satisfied. She will awake at all hours of the night with a twinge of her ghost pain, which she will then seek to soothe with a comforting touch. Touch will turn to caress, and then she will be lost, tossing and turning, with her fingers wetly busy between her legs until dawn.

"The same thing will certainly happen to her in her bath. An innocent effort at cleanliness will result in an veritable orgy of passion that she will be utterly powerless to resist. She will have to be physically carried from her tub, so delighted will she be with the masturbatory opportunities it provides her. She would remain at it all day otherwise!"

When I seemed doubtful about this, Mlle. T. smiled, somewhat indulgently, and made a sign to Jo Lin, who, in response, removed the cover from a small porcelain jar on her tray, extracting a dollop of what appeared to be some exotic variety of scented cream. She proceeded to apply this preparation gently to the sensitive, reddened

lips of sex of the girl who was the subject of our conversation.

Beverly reacted with a start, bucking violently against her restraints, no doubt believing that her ordeal was not yet over, and was now to be continued. This startled reaction was soon transformed, however, into a simple, slight shifting to and fro of her hips, as far as the still tightly bound young girl was able to move them.

"Mmmmmm." Beverly released a small moan, which was barely audible.

Then, as Jo Lin's caresses became somewhat more insistent, there came a shuddering exhalation, followed by a heaving intake of breath... a pause... and then a scream that fully equaled those we had previously heard only in response to her most intense discomfort. It was a scream of absolute, unrestrained orgasm.

With that, the girl collapsed once more into unconsciousness.

Mlle. T. gave me a look of pride at the vindication of her claims. "Our Beverly's young body will soon learn to endure such intense pleasures without lapsing into insensitivity. Then, for a time, she will sleep only when completely, hopelessly overcome with exhaustion."

She chuckled, "She will be quite a little noise-maker until then, though. Karl, we must place Beverly in one of the silent rooms for a few days, so that her cries at self-play will not disturb our other students. See that she has food and water when, and if, she wants it."

The servant nodded and, with an approving nod to Jo Lin, and with a final affectionate glance at the unconscious Beverly, Mlle. T. led me from the room.

Mlle. T. escorted me along the many twisting corridors back to my own bed chamber, where she soon took leave of me, and where I lay down instantly upon the welcoming bed, exhausted by all I had seen on this, the first day of my visit to the Chateau Noir.

CHAPTER SIX - TRAINING

I spent my second day at the Chateau Noir in touring what Mlle. T. referred to as her "training chambers", these being several rooms scattered throughout the building that had each been furnished and appointed according to its own specific purpose. There were chambers fitted out in the finest luxury, and then again there were those which were styled more to the tastes of the strictest of Spartans.

One large room, this upon the building's ground floor, I perceived to have once been a music room, as it included among its decorations and appointments several ornate and antique music stands, large bookshelves upon which there were still stored tall stacks of printed music. There was even a small harpsichord, standing closed and silent in one corner.

In this room also, upon the deep, plush oriental carpeting, no doubt originally laid for the purpose of absorbing the harsher reverberations a bare wooden floor would

have merely amplified, stood a long, narrow table of heavy wood. And stretched naked, belly down, along this table, and bent sharply forward at her waist, another of Mlle. T.'s young students, a blonde-haired nymph of about sixteen, had been tightly bound.

The girl's legs were held widely spread apart and her ankles tightly strapped to the legs of the table at one end. Other tight straps extending from the opposite end of the table and fixed about the girl's wrists served to stretch her body to the tautness of a bowstring.

Behind the bound girl there stood the manservant Karl, a long, black leather buggy whip in his hand. This whip he was vigorously applying to the young girl's naked backside in firm, regular, solid strokes that cut the air with a audible whooshing sound before cutting into the girl's soft bottom-flesh with a sharp, cracking report that was, in turn, followed close by a gasping, wailing shriek from the girl herself.

These punishing strokes were spaced well apart, however, measured out according to the voice of a small, golden clock, about seven inches tall and encrusted with bright

jewels, that had been set to chime once with the passing of each minute.

Upon this regularly paced chiming of the clock, the whip would descend with the same whoosh and crack I have described. And after each cruel stroke had been delivered, the tormented girl's sharp cry of intense discomfort would erupt and then subside into soft, tearful sobs, as she stared into the unsympathetic visage of the clock and endured the fearful wait as the next minute swiftly ticked past.

"It is a lesson in anticipation," Mlle. T. murmured, quietly. "By the regular striking of the clock, by knowing, to the second, precisely when she may expect the next bright pulse of pain, the girl is learning to experience her discomfort to the fullest, and thereby will soon know, by pure instinct, to apply that same capacity for anticipation to the more exquisite experience of pleasure."

Mlle. T.'s remarks were here punctuated by another crystalline chiming of the clock, the cracking report of the buggy whip and, finally, the alarmed cry of the tortured young girl, this cry somewhat louder than before. My position, to the rear of the student being trained, offered an unobscured view of the sweetly proffered

backside, and I could readily observe the clenching and working of the girl's flanks as she responded to the whip's crashing stroke and then awaited in dreadful anticipation of the next. The halved pear of the tender sex of the young girl seemed to open and close, winkingly, as did that more secret, lower, nether opening, as if in complete disregard for the lascivious display these movements presented to those present. The discomfort of the ordeal must, indeed, have been severe to so obscure in the young girl any thoughts of the immodesty of her position.

"The sensation intensifies with each stroke, and with each minute of the girl's anticipation, do you see?" said Mlle. T. "She has endured but her first few minutes. This lesson is stipulated to last for a full hour. Soon she will be at the bare edge of her mind's ability to even perceive her discomfort. It will all, by hour's end, become one with her. She will, of course, have to be more tightly bound at that point than she is now, her fingers wrapped in cloth so that she will not damage the table's finish with the clawing of her nails, and her mouth properly bitted to prevent damage to her sweet tongue."

The next stroke of the leather against the girl's backside occasioned just such a response as Mlle. T. had been predicting. The girl now made a desperate effort to free herself from her bonds, wrenching fiercely about, what little she was able, until Mlle. T. motioned for Karl to take the precautions she has described. The bitting of the girl's mouth, the wrapping of her hands and the tightening of the strong leather straps were all accomplished in less that a minute, so that the lesson was resumed with no respite beyond the single minute prescribed.

Again, with the circuit of the clock's small second hand to the top of the numbered face, the indefatigable Karl swung the buggy whip widely out and back, winding up to once again bring the length of supple, black leather and bamboo snapping viciously into the soft, curving flesh of the now most repentant young girl bent helplessly before him, at nearly the same instant as the clock emitted its coldly innocent and uncaringly chiming "ping." And, again, the girl erupted as before with the same frantic grunting squeals of desperation and bitter struggling against her unyielding bonds.

There was something almost calming in the observation of this process that is difficult for me to describe even now. Somehow, though one could not escape identifying with the unpleasant plight of the girl undergoing this extreme form of punishment - one could easily discern, for instance, from her panicked cries, the discomfort she was undergoing under the servant's harsh, regular lashing - there was something in the very regularity of those punishing strokes that proved somehow soothing to those observing the process.

At the time, I looked about me, into the countenances of both the administrator of the painfully whipping strokes and the woman who had ordered them, and could see either face nothing other than a quite serenity. There was no glint of salaciousness about the eye, as might have been suspected in one who might actually relish, in a voyeuristic manner, the scene they were both witness to and participants in. There was not the slightest hint of empathy, no flinch of muscle at the sharp cracking report of leather against female bottom-flesh that might signal any regretful affinity with the girl's obvious torment.

In the faces of both Karl and Mlle. T. there was but an expression of certain, glowing calm, a radiant peace that pervaded all. And I soon found myself as well falling under the same spell that mesmerized these others, lured into a strange, calm, and undeniably pleasant peacefulness which progressed unaccountably with the regularity of the ticking clock there on the table and the tolling of the bell and punishing whiplash that came inexorably with each sixty second interval that passed.

Chime, whip, scream. The ticking of the clock, the whimper of anticipation from the blonde sixteen-year-old. Chime, whip, scream. On and on, for exactly how long I am uncertain. But the endurance of the young girl was impressive.

My reverie was broken as a meaningful glance passed between Karl and his mistress just as the student being dealt with yelped at the most recent chiming of the clock and the snapping blow of the buggy whip across her trembling young mounds that so closely followed. And a second afterward, just as the girl had begun to relax for the blessed sixty-second interval of reprieve before the next anticipated crashing blow, the servant Karl exploded into a whirr of motion,

planting upwards of ten to perhaps fifteen rapid-fire strokes of the whip along both cheeks of the girl's divided rump.

The student detonated into a frenzy. The paneled walls of the music room echoed, reverberated and rang with the shrillness of the surprised betrayal of the young girl. She shrieked around the gagging bit between her teeth, her mouth and eyes widely opened in wild panic, and her entire frame bucked upwards against the leather restraints, howling and writhing for the duration of Karl's furious and wholly unexpected attack.

It was as if a thousand wasps had taken the few seconds the dozen or so strokes required to plunge their venomous stingers all at once into various points along the sweet curves of soft woman-flesh, causing the poor thing a combined agony the possibility of which the previous widely spaced strokes could only have suggested.

When, at last, the quick, cracking flurry of shocks gave way, the girl's tearful shrieks carried on, for having once been betrayed as to the rules of her ordeal the girl could not now be entirely certain some new, and even more exquisitely painful surprise awaited her.

But after a moment all was silent, save for the ticking of the small jeweled clock and the gasping, sniffling sobs of the girl as her panicked cries finally subsided.

As I watched, Mlle. T. nodded to her servant, indicating her satisfaction with this proper performance of his duties. Karl, betraying as always not the slightest hit of emotion, of sympathy or otherwise, calmly and wordlessly placed the well used buggy whip upon the wall rack where it apparently belonged. This was a kind of storage unit similar to racks commonly seen in billiard rooms, designed for the storage of cue sticks, and the space in which Karl placed the instrument was the only niche remaining unoccupied by brother and sister appliances of the same nature.

The rack held whips of all sizes and materials, as I noted some time later, when I had leisure to examine its contents more closely. There were long, thin rods bound in supple leather such as might be seen in use in the finest stable yards. There were also various lengths of new cane, polished and glistening with fresh varnish, or wax. Mlle. T. mentioned on that later occasion that a waxed cane offered a sensation upon the backside or breasts of an errant female as

different from that of a like instrument layered in varnish as the taste of salt is distinguishable from that of sugar.

As I have said, the wild cries of the young girl strapped to the music room table had ceased to assail our ears as it became understood to her that the stinging smacks of Karl's buggy whip had, at least for the moment, ceased to assail the burning flesh of her tender rump. All that could be heard now were the quiet sounds of the girl's tearful, sniffling sobs as she attempted, only somewhat successfully, to recover her composure.

Mlle. T., however, took this very moment to interfere with the girl's efforts at self-control by approaching the young student from behind and placing one hand, palm downwards, upon the glowing redness of the girl's lined and whelp-covered left rear cheek. Approaching, as I say, from behind, this touch came as a complete surprise to the girl, and as the touch appeared to be most gentle and soothing, I was startled by the student's precipitous reaction. At the first gentle contact of hand against rump the girl bucked upwards against her restraints and again screamed wildly around the hard

rubber bit as if Karl's punishing whip strokes had abruptly begun anew.

It was, I believe, a combination of surprise at the unexpected touch and a very real tenderness of the darkly flushed and redly marked rump-flesh that caused the girl's fearful reaction, for now, having realized that her Karl's "instruction" was for the moment done - she had watched with obvious relief as the man had passed out through a door within her view - and as Mlle. T.'s touches rapidly demonstrated themselves to be only the tenderest of caresses, the girl's panic once again subsided.

Gentle palm and fingertips now lightly brushed and stroked the red-hot looking curves of girlish buttocks with a soothing and calming regularity. Small sobs and tearful sniffles soon gave way to quiet whimpers begging sympathy from her harsh Mistress.

Continuing her ministrations, Mlle. T. turned to me and motioned me forward. I came to her side, trying to avoid staring directly at this delectable, closer view of the student's openly exposed sex. Mlle. T. caught my embarrassed glance and smiled, somewhat chidingly, diverting my eyes

again to the very object I had endeavoured to modestly ignore.

The lightly furred peach of the girl's young sex stood open before me, the lips still slightly parted as a result of the contortive gymnastics her lithe figure had performed moments earlier under the lash, a young girl's unpainted pink lips parted with breathless excitement in anticipation of her very first kiss. The wispy blonde curls fringing the delicious aperture added a gentle sweetness to the sight, and the solitary eye of that tightly closed rosebud above appeared strangely even sweeter in its particular exposed vulnerability. Another quietly amused glance from Mlle. T. invited me to a closer inspection, this time by way of direct touch. The firm right hand of the Mistress of the Chateau Noir gathered in my own, as the palm and fingers of her left continued to lightly stroke the curves of the abused young cheeks. Reluctantly I allowed my hand to be placed upon the soft right half of the girl's tender rump. The young blonde caught her breath as this stranger's palm settled onto the sensitive flesh. I glanced up along the narrow range of her bare back to catch her looking over her right shoulder at me, my eyes caught for an instant by her two

tear-filled pools of deepest blue beneath the short golden bangs plastered to a somewhat darker shade by the perspiration that wetted her forehead. There was a hit of weary exhaustion there, and something more, an emotion I could not quite read. The lips around the hard rubber of the bit seemed relaxed now and the face appeared calmer than before. One interlocking glance, and then the girl turned away to rest her head, left cheek downward against the smooth-varnished surface of the table to which she was bound.

The female flesh seemed to burn my open palm with it's heat, the redness of the punished rear cheek radiating outward to cause a sympathetic vibration within my own system. I felt the girl's painfully throbbing as if it were my own. The numerous interlocking welts that criss-crossed the tender curve of delicate flesh told in a language even a blind man could readily decipher.

I gently traced one of these lines from in-turning centre valley on outward to the girl's side, where it at last came to an end, and I imagined I felt the single, lashing stroke of the whip that had written there its tale of bright, flashing torment, now replaced by a

pulsing heat in the aftermath, the healing of the female flesh already begun.

Mlle. T. again directed my gaze downward into the sweet divide of the young girl's rear. The woman leaned close in, to whisper briefly in my left ear." Remember. With pain must always come pleasure. That is the lesson we impart here. No matter what unpleasant torments the lives of these girls hold in store in the future, it is the pleasure, the deliciously intense pleasures they are here learning to give, and to receive, that must become the centre of all their attention. Soon, with careful training, each with learn to dismiss the former and embrace the latter. When they have mastered that, there in no unpleasantness they will not be able to overcome. They will become the mistresses of their own lives, and more."

I must have looked as if I were about to respond with a whispered request for some clarification on this point - which I was, indeed, later on to learn was the true heart, soul and secret of the Chateau Noir and of Mlle. T.'s philosophy - for the Mistress immediately silenced my coming inquiries with another communicative glance.

Once more she directed my attention to the posterior of the girl strapped prone

before us. Mlle. T.'s caresses continued as they had throughout the preceding few moments, but now her long, tender strokes seemed to be progressing ever downwards into the crevice that separated the girl's lusciously reddened bottom-cheeks, fingertips now and again venturing into the sweet divide itself, now, at last, brushing lightly against the outer ridges that formed the delicate lips of the female sex itself.

I saw the muscles along the back of the young girl tense at this, and there was a small sigh from her bitted lips, barely audible from where we stood.

The next instant drew a small, sharp cry of, "Oh!" from the girl, drawing my attention again to Mlle. T.'s caressing fingers, which I noted had now parted the tender lips of the young blonde's inner sex. One fingertip had entered a fraction into the interior of that sweet channel, and was now toying mischievously with the delicate flesh just inside.

"Oh!" the girl cried again, as I saw Mlle. T.'s efforts rewarded with a sudden flow of wetness at the lower boundary of the girlish opening, a small spring beginning to flow outward there, tricking downward toward the electric button of the girl's clitoris, which

was beginning to poke its small head out from under its protective hood in curiosity, seeming to invite a further, deeper exploration to the secret source of that flow.

"Mmmmmmmmmmmmmmm," the girl whined, in a highly-pitched tone, her narrow hips now beginning a slight, slow writhing under her mistress's touch.

Mlle. T.'s fingers were now teasing lower along her student's now wetly parted love lips, and in a moment it was the girl's small clit itself that was being manipulated and stroked as the mistress worked expertly to coax the little nub more and more into view.

"Ohhhhhhhhhh! Ohhhhhhhhhhh!" The girl was becoming more animated now in her movements in response to the older woman's fondlings, her hips writhing so that it was only through careful attention to those frantic motions that the Mistress was able to maintain constant teasing contact with the small target of her manipulations.

It was clear that the young blonde was approaching a sexual climax under the masturbatory hand of her knowledgeable instructress, her entire body now overcome by a frenzy of erratic motion, hips nearly awhirl before us, back arching upwards as if

she were a young mare being mounted for the very first time by a rampant young stallion.

Her blonde hair tossed in a deranged manner, first backwards, as her head arched upwards in response to some delectably delightful caress from her Mistress's fingers against the small bud of her clitoris, then forward, shrouding her face in a golden curtain, a yellow veil of silken tresses momentarily concealing a facial expression of wild, tormented passion, then all at once that long, golden hair was whipping from side to side in a frantic blur as the poor girl's passion threatened to reach it's final, unsurpassable peak.

"No. Nooooooo!" A small denial, then a panicked, begging, pleading, caterwauling cry to the gods as that passionate peak finally overcame her.

The walls of the music room rang once more with a wild, girlish shriek of unendurable emotion, this current cry of sweet, passionate pleasure as piercing as the cries of horrible pain which had preceded it but a short while earlier, and no doubt the pleasure of this present moment was as intense and exquisitely powerful as had been

that earlier torment, for the girl's physical reactions appeared remarkably the same.

The observation of this fact brought me once again to the very brink of understanding another of Mlle. T.'s training principals, the almost mystical relationship - indeed, the intimate correlation - between the subtle and primitive experiences and essences of pleasure and pain.

The young student bound before us continued to writhe and cry out in mounting shrieks of painful, pleasurable anticipation until, her body tensing suddenly and silently for a single trembling instant, she exploded into a convulsive, all-consuming and undeniable orgasm.

She shrieked, her high, mournful howl to the heavens surpassing even the cries she had given at Karl's final barrage of whip strokes at the conclusion of her preceding ordeal. For nearly a full minute her cries assailed our ears, as the girl's earth-shattering come continued unabated until, her endurance at a frazzled end, with one last, final, exhausting scream the little blonde sixteen-year-old collapsed into a spontaneous unconsciousness, her body sagging, insensible, against the perspiration-soaked surface of the long table.

I watched as Mlle. T. calmly withdrew her hand from the valley of flesh she had been so pleasurably tormenting, her hand now wet with the freshly pooling, lubricating juices of the girl's rampant spend. She wiped her hands methodically upon a red silk handkerchief she pulled from somewhere about her person and stood for a moment, calmly gazing at the fainted young girl.

"Karl will awaken her in a few moments," she said. In the quiet of the aftermath the ticking of the small clock was again detectable over the sound of the unconscious girl's ragged breathing. "Then her instruction will begin again."

I imagined with surprise and awe the young student's despair at being awakened to find that her ordeal had but begun.

I myself, however, was not to witness this awakening and resumption. Mlle. T. informed me in the next moment that my tour of the Chateau's training rooms was now to continue.

CHAPTER SEVEN - THE WATER-CLOCK

Time. As I reflect back upon my days at the Chateau Noir, I am arrested by the images and symbols of time that surrounded me always. The clocks, which seemed to be everywhere, upon mantels, in the girl's bed chambers, in the long, meandering hallways and in the secret passages winding throughout the building. Even the neighbouring stables were equipped with timepieces of one kind or another.

And apart from this, the ever present reminders that time, as well as the regimentally designed and controlled experiences of the girls at the Chateau Noir, was bringing subtle changes in the girls themselves. The slow, gradual, almost imperceptible changes from young girlhood into blooming young womanhood, the swelling of breasts and hips to the riper fullness of approaching maturity, the darkening of bright countenances as age and experience carried the students at the

Chateau from the sparkle of fresh innocence through the slight, unavoidable tarnish of gained experience and knowledge and then, finally, into the full and fruitful blossoming of real awareness of the true and irresistible power of the female sex.

But I am getting ahead of my story, for none of the truths, none of the real truths about Mlle. T.'s purposes at the Chateau Noir had become known to me at the time of this, my first morning's tour of the school's training rooms.

Having left the beautiful young blonde student of the events of the preceding chapter resting in preparation for another session under the lash, I followed Mlle. T. through a small passage connecting the Chateau's music room with another, much larger chamber beyond. Like the room we had just vacated, this chamber was paneled in dark, polished wood, but unlike the other room the walls of this chamber also appeared to have been lined with cork at certain points. Oddly shaped squares and ovals of this material had been inlaid here and there. Mlle. T. offered an explanation for this some time later. The sections of cork had been placed upon the walls as a means of dampening down the acoustics of

the room. As a result of these installations, even the sharpest, most piercing cries uttered within this chamber would amount to but the tiniest of squeaks if heard from outside the building.

I say that Mlle. T. offered this explanation of the room's unusual-looking decorations at a later occasion. That is because when I first entered this particular room my attentions were exclusively drawn to a truly extraordinary apparatus that had been constructed upon its northernmost wall.

This machine consisted of a huge wooden frame, the dark wood of which appeared to have been polished to a smooth, rich gleaming finish that glowed warmly in the candlelight, for the room had no windows at all in the high paneled and cork lined walls and so, the bright sunlight of autumn from without having been sealed away, candles provided the only light within. These candles stood in elaborately wrought artifices of iron, standing at each of the room's for corners, and holding the shafts of at least a dozen candles each.

Apart from the aforementioned massive frame of polished wood, so massive, indeed, that it appeared to have been securely, and necessarily, anchored to both floor and

ceiling with a series of equally massive iron bolts, the device consisted of a mysterious conglomeration of interlocking cogs and wide leather belts running in a circular confusion, the design of which I found completely unfathomable.

Centred at the top of this amazing apparatus was a large wooden clock face nearly three feet in circumference, the hands of which, both hour and minute, were currently joined straight up at the number "Twelve" painted in black Roman numerals, as were all the symbols upon the clock's polished face. The hands of the clock were not in motion at the moment, as I discerned from glancing up at the face a moment or so later as my examination of this baffling device continued.

Also near the ceiling of the room's north wall I noticed a configuration of tubes and water pipes descending from just below the ceiling and running downward until they were lost in the confusion of the apparatus itself. The uppermost pipe opened out into a sort of funnel just below the ceiling, and just above this upturned funnel I now took note of a small hole in the ceiling itself. Both funnel and the hole under which it had been

arranged appeared to be somewhat water-stained.

The lower portion of the complicated apparatus consisted of a sort of table, upholstered and padded in dark, well-worn leather to which leather straps had been bolted in a configuration much like on other such tables I would see elsewhere in the various other training rooms at the Chateau.

At one end of this table and leveled an inch or so above its surface there appeared to have been positioned a long, smooth shaft of what looked like the finest, polished steel, nearly three feet in its total length as it protruded from the clockwork of the machine and extended over the end of the leather-padded table for the final foot of that length. This smooth, metal shaft, which gleamed mirror-like in the candlelight, tapered from a three-inch width at its source, where it disappeared within the machinery to about an inch at its rounded near extremity, that being the portion which overlapped the table.

Mlle. T. stepped toward the huge device and with a knowing hand sought out a small hand-crank beneath the foot of the padded table. There was a well-oiled, but slightly ratchety sound as she turned this crank and,

as I watched, the aforementioned steel shaft slowly withdrew its protruding length, which a moment before had overlapped that end of the table. With a final turn of the crank the shaft was now drawn back to two or three inches beyond the table's edge. Mlle. T., still offering no explanations, then stood back and returned casually to my side.

As I say, the purpose for such a bizarre apparatus was a complete and utter mystery to me, even as I now stood before it, Mlle. T. close by my side, the lady no doubt bemused by my mystification.

The mystery was not prolonged, however, for a moment or two later that other servant at the Chateau, the hitherto unseen Alex, son or brother to Karl, arrived at the chamber's other door, an apparently hidden panel opening into the room at its right-hand wall. With the servant was a beautiful, dark-haired woman of about twenty, dressed in the usual student uniform of short white tunic. Her raven tresses fell well beyond her white shoulders, bare but for the single narrow shoulder strap which held the tunic in place. There was a sheen to these long, dark wavelets which seemed to glow with an inner light all its own, and her face held a certain indefinable calm which I

had to that point seen in none of Mlle. T.'s students before. From her age, and from this self-possessed demeanour, I guessed this young woman to be one of Mlle. T.'s more advanced pupils.

Alex led the young woman forward. Standing at the head of the padded table, she stood motionless as the servant loosed the shoulder strap of her tunic and the woman let it fall heedlessly to the floor about her feet. With Alex's assistance she then stepped away from the puddle of white silk and turned to seat herself upon the edge of the padded table. Alex's strong-looking hands gently but firmly guided the young woman into a supine position, her fine bottom centred nearly at the table's edge facing the huge cluster of machinery I have described, her legs drawn up and supported for the moment by her heels.

The servant busied himself for a few moments with the various straps which were fixed to both the table itself and which also hung from each side of a wooden frame which stood overlooking the table's foot. Soon the dark-haired beauty lay strapped down to the table, her wrists shackled into soft, but strong-looking leather cuffs fixed with silver buckles that drew her hands and

arms back above her, her head now rested upon a sort of leather bolster that served to raised her so that her gaze could readily take in the complicated mechanism arranged before her.

The woman's heels, which at this point remained resting upon the padded table's edge, were now lifted by Alex into the waiting ankle cuffs which hung from the two straps suspended from the wooden framework above. Yet another crank, this one fixed to one side of this framework was now employed by Alex to reel these two leg straps slowly upward until the woman's thighs were drawn into a taught, spread-eagle position, her hips resting at the bare edge of the table and her legs separated in a wide, upright "V" position at right angles to her reclining torso.

One more measure was apparently necessary before whatever was about to occur could begin. Three wide leather straps were now drawn across the young woman's reclining form from left to right, two positioned over her bare chest, one just above and the other just below her ripe bosom, causing these twin globes to lift themselves even more proudly than had been their want. And the third of these strong

leather body cuffs was drawn across the young woman's belly or, more precisely, just below that gentle rise and just above the proud jut of her full, feminine hips.

All three of these restraining straps were then cinched tight, so tight in fact that for the first time I noted the slightest hint of reaction from the young woman, who until now had appeared a perfect study of aloofness. Now she gasped audibly as the twin straps framing her breasts from above and below were forced upward and outward from the combined pressure. I noted that this pressure had also precipitated a tightness within those sweet girl-fruits themselves, causing the small berries of her nipples to ripen into such an erect hardness that it must have been somewhat painful for the girl who bore them.

The combined effect of all these restraints was that the dark-haired young woman was fixed tightly to the padded table before us, motionless, completely incapable of movement, no matter what fate should befall her.

Mlle. T.'s soft voice, now cold again as always when in the presence of any of her students, spoke at this point for the first time since we had entered the room.

"This," she said, indicating the machinery that her bound young student now faced before her, framed between her own widely splayed legs, "This... is our water-clock. It is a design of our own, ingenious Alex. A wonder of invention, is our Alex. Though it took him nearly a year to perfect the device."

There was not the slightest change of expression, not the slightest hint of pleasure or satisfaction from the tall man at his Mistress's kind words of praise. He merely continued moving about the machinery that made up his device, his "water-clock." He tightened a fitting here, adjusted a setting there, as if her were some factory worker left on his own, dedicated to his job, quietly capable of running the apparatus up to his own, careful, competent specification, with or without the approval or unneeded supervision from management.

"The principle of the device is simple," Mlle. T. continued. "You will notice the small opening in the ceiling, just above the intake funnel."

I looked upwards to the water-stained opening and funnel-shaped pipe end I had taken notice of earlier. "That opening is connected, through a series of sluices and

conduits, to the fresh-water spring which flows near the rear of this main building. A lever here within this chamber can be shifted to allow water from that spring to be channeled at a varying rate of flow through that aperture in the ceiling and into the pipe-work of the clock below. The water then drives the mechanism at varying speeds accordingly."

I looked at Mlle. T., who at that moment had glanced toward me. My remaining lack of understanding must have been clear upon my face, for she nodded reassuringly, indicating that I should be patient and that all would be clear in good time.

"This particular student," said Mlle. T. as our silent exchange was completed, "is undergoing a series of treatments designed to enable her young body to withstand the rigours of extended copulation. The gentleman who has enlisted her services upon completion of her education here has specified his tastes to me very clearly, as I insist all our clients do, for how can I hope to perfect our training regimes to the satisfaction of each of our client's needs if I do not clearly understand what those needs are?"

Mlle. T. approached the head of the table to which the pupil in question had been strapped. She lay the cool fingers of one hand upon the brow of the dark-haired beauty, stroking the few stray commas of silken night away and to the side as she continued to speak.

"Melody was this creature's name, though she has no name at all now. Her new master has expressed his wish to christen her himself when she is delivered up to him. We shall comply. We have also complied with this gentleman's wish that his new acquisition be capable, on occasion, of enjoying - of surviving, as he puts it - quite a large number of male sexual partners, in rapid succession, sometimes up to a ten or so at a time. Apparently this particular client enjoys the pleasures of voyeurism above all others."

Mlle. T. smiled somewhat tightly. "I myself suspect that he secretly wishes to break the spirit of this, his new courtesan. There are men like that in the world, you know. But I believe he will find such a goal very difficult to attain in the case of our Melody, here, for she will come to him, when she does so, completely capable of taking on partners by the dozens without

complaint. Fifty rampant males will not break this one. In fact, even now, with her training as yet incomplete, she could accept the plunging of dozen male members to their utter exhaustion and be quite fresh and ready for a dozen more. And when her time here at the school is done, a hundred mountings will not phase her."

There was an unquestioned expression of pride in the countenance of Mlle. T. as she said these words, and I felt a growing understanding of the fierce pride the Mistress of the Chateau Noir felt for her students, for all the effort she made, for discipline's sake, to shield this from her charges. Probably she only allowed herself to speak with such openness before this particular student now because the dark-haired Melody's training was, as I gleaned from the content of her remarks, nearly complete, and so nothing was to be lost from such candour at this point.

But still I was increasingly anxious to learn the precise nature of the training ordeal I was apparently now to witness. What had this "water-clock" to do with maximizing the sexual endurance level of the young woman lying bound before us?

My answer came with but a few more moment's delay. Mlle. T. applied a final, almost loving, caress to the brow of her young student, and then nodded perfunctorily to Alex, who had finished with his adjustments and tunings to the instrumentation of his mechanism and now stood patiently awaiting his Mistress's command.

The servant came forward and approached a large lever set against a side wall. With some effort he moved this lever slightly from the left to the right, so that the wooden shaft of the lever was aligned to the first of several various markings upon the wall to which it was fixed. There was a slight rushing, the sound of water I guessed, the water flowing from the fresh-water spring Mlle. T. had described. And a second or two later a moderate trickle of this clear liquid began to flow from out the hole in the ceiling above and to fall down into the waiting funnel end of the upturned intake pipe of the water-clock.

There was a sound of movement, first a grating of machinery coming reluctantly to life, then a soft, groaning rumble as the full mechanism of the clock began to come into motion. Gears turned against gears, wide

leather belts turned huge wooden wheels, and all the while there was that rushing gurgle of water flowing throughout the mechanism like blood pumping through the body of a living being. For the machine was, in a sense, alive now, churning and pulsing, though in the creaky, stiff manner of some ancient turning out for his accustomed morning stroll, his joints and muscles protesting, still stiff from sleep.

Alex, father of this machine, sprang about making some further adjustments, adding the lubrication of some oily looking substance where needed, and soon the complaining creaks and groans of the contraption were replaced by a smooth, untroubled rumble of quietly controlled power.

But still I could not for the life of me ascertain the purpose of the mechanism. That is, until my eyes were drawn to what Mlle. T. was now doing by the foot of the table near the upturned "V" of her student's widely splayed legs. My curiosity overcame my timidity, and I moved closer to see at what task Mlle. T. was now occupied.

What I now saw was Mlle. T. briskly, though carefully, applying some sort of thick, clear substance at the joining of the

young woman's parted thighs. I blushed to see her at work so diligently with a small brush, spreading this substance assiduously around, and even between, the intimate lips of the sex of her pupil.

The foliage surrounding the girl's nether openings had been carefully shaved, or perhaps plucked, as I had seen the much younger Beverly plucked just the night before, and the clear substance now being applied to the smooth, delicate woman-flesh seemed to cling wetly to where it was brushed.

I looked toward the upturned face of the young woman being so intimately attended to and saw in those moist, night-dark eyes an expression that communicated a subtle mix of pleasure at these intimate, brushing caresses, and a note, as well, of carefully contained anxiety, no doubt in anticipation of whatever ordeal lay immediately before her.

Mlle. T. noticed my presence at her shoulder and spoke quietly to me in explanation. "It is a preparation, Thomas, a lubricant, that I have designed myself for this particular procedure, a mixture of natural vegetable oils pressed from almonds and various other ingredients. I have found

it superior to all other substitutes, especially for its lasting quality. It is not absorbed too quickly by the skin, nor does it evaporate over long periods of time, and therefore it does not require replenishing as often as most. That is particularly important in the procedure you are about to witness."

It was now that the true nature and purpose of Alex's water-clock suddenly became clear to me, as I happened to glance away from the pink, tantalizing delights now wetly open between the dark-haired Melody's widely spread thighs, which had held my gaze like a magnet will draw iron, and into the gleam of the polished steel shaft, which I have described as positioned parallel to and just above the table's padded surface had come into motion through the mechanism of the clock. The gleaming rod was now moving smoothly and silently back and forth in an unmistakably thrusting manner. One glance from the smooth, rounded tip of this rod to the now luxuriously lubricated orifice of flesh at which it was aimed left no doubt in my mind whatsoever as for the purpose of Alex's miraculous water-clock and the "training" ordeal the raven-haired beauty upon the table was about to endure.

I stared from the rod of steel to vulnerably exposed underflesh of the young woman as if transfixed, mesmerized. I knew what was going to happen and felt myself aroused at the prospect of seeing it happen as nothing I had seen at the Chateau Noir had done before.

Having apparently satisfied herself as to the adequacy of the state of her young student's sexual lubrication, Mlle. T. withdrew her brush and returned it, along with the jar containing the oily preparation, to a small cabinet set in the room's left-hand wall. Back at the foot of the padded table now, she reached below to the small hand-crank I mentioned before, the one which she had used to cause the steel rod of the mechanism to retract away from the table's end. A reverse rotation of this crank had the expected effect of reversing that action, and now every turn of Mlle. T.'s firm hand brought the aggressively thrusting shaft an inch or so closer to the waiting mouth of Melody's tender sex.

I looked to the face of the girl to ascertain her attitude as the moment of her inevitable violation grew ever nearer, and saw in that face only the slightest hint of anxiety. It was perhaps true that there was

more of an excited anticipation there than actual fear. But whether of pleasure or of discomfort there certainly seemed there a definite knowledge of an ordeal soon to be undergone and endured. Later I was to learn that the young woman had, in fact, undergone this training ritual at least three times previously, so it was true that the girl did, indeed, know full well the rigours of the ordeal about to befall her.

Closer and ever closer came the rounded tip of the trusting shaft of metal. Now each inward thrust came within a single inch of making actual contact with the delicate lips which awaited its intrusion. The girl at this point had begun to tremble a bit, her upturned face becoming tightly closed, her emotions contained with much outwardly displayed effort and determination. Her lower lip was caught tentatively between her teeth, her eyes frozen to the pulsing movement of the approaching steel.

Mlle. T. watched the girl's expression as well, judging for herself the exact moment when that crucial turn of the crank would bring the tip of the metal phallus plunging into the waiting girl-lips and into the sweet channel beyond.

That moment arrived. With a slow twist of her wrist, Mlle. T. performed the final necessary movement of the crank, and at it's very next thrust the glittering steel of the shaft... touched... and... penetrated... the glistening wet opening which had stood tremblingly awaiting it.

The girl gasped audibly at this initial intrusion, for it occurred to me at that moment that the metal rod must be somewhat cold, especially as applied to the warmly intimate flesh of the girl's most tender part. But, as this first thrust only penetrated that delicious part only to the shallow depth of but a half an inch, the girl's gasping reaction could not as yet have been caused by any more serious discomfort.

My suspicions proved well founded, for with the application of ten or so additional thrusts at the same limited level of intrusion the girl became somewhat used to steel's cold insinuation, or perhaps the intense heat from within the girl herself served to reduce the chill of the metal to a more endurable temperature. At any rate, the young woman seemed to settle down to the regular repetition of the rod's intrusion until the point was reached where there was no reaction to the metal's thrusting at all.

After a few moments of this, Mlle. T. addressed the reclining girl. "Are you ready, Melody?" she asked. The girl paused but a moment and then, setting her teeth and bracing her body for what was to come, she nodded shortly. "Very well," said Mlle. T. and began again slowly to turn the crank.

Slowly, ever so slowly, the thrusting of the metal slipped farther into the open loins of the young woman. First a single inch of depth was attained, then two, then three. Melody seemed now to be straining somewhat against her bonds, not in an effort to escape the oncoming thrusts, it appeared, but to brace herself more fully to withstand the carnal sensations such intimate intrusion was certain to arouse.

Another slow inch, then another, and then the plunging rod of steel was sinking with each extremity of its penetration to the depth of seven full inches into the trembling tunnel of the young woman's flesh.

Melody was incapable of suppressing her emotions now. Each thrust brought an low, gasping grunt of effort form the girl. Her legs shivered and strained in the leather straps which held them so tightly aloft. Her toes alternately pointed, then curled as sensations seemed to roll outward from her

violated sex in waves of pure, electric excitement that shivered and vibrated now throughout her entire frame.

Mlle. T. quietly noted these reactions, and all the while continued with the slow, steady turning of the crank until, at the penetration level I estimated at about ten full inches, young Melody's attempt at quiet calm seemed to break down with a sudden exclamation.

"N...noooooooooooooo!" She screamed. It was not, however, a cry of pain. It was, instead, the sound which heralded the approach of girl's first orgasm under the stimulation of the water-clock.

Then the girl screamed out in earnest, in a full, soul wrenching girl-cum. The high rafters of the chamber rang and reverberated with the mournful, piercing shriek. The sound set the small hairs at the back of my neck erect, and caused the faint shadow of a smile to appear upon the tight red lips of Mlle. T. It was smile of knowing admiration.

Melody's cries of passion continued for some minutes as the intensity of her orgasm maintained it's high, timorous peak, the limbs of the young woman convulsing uncontrollably within her bonds all the

while. And all the while the working of the mechanism of the water-clock and the thrusting of its smooth metal shaft maintained its slow, measured penetrations.

Finally the young woman's orgasm seemed to have run its course. All at once she sagged back against the padded table, her body suddenly slack within her binding straps. There was a fine patina of sweet perspiration covering the alabaster whiteness of her skin. The tossing of her head during climax had scattered a few wisps of her dark hair back across her perspiration-damp forehead where they now lay plastered in that sweet moisture. The dark eyes of the girl were closed in an almost peaceful repose, but flew open again at second later in abrupt alarm.

What had happened? I soon saw. Mlle. T. had selected that very moment of repose, the dropping of the young woman's guard, to apply several additional quick turns of the control crank, sending the smooth metal of the plunging shaft up inside the girl to an total increased depth of nearly fifteen inches.

The girl erupted into a true frenzy of emotion, calling out to her Mistress in frantic, wordless pleas for mercy. The steel shaft of the water-clock's false phallus had

been designed, as I have described, not only to be of great length but also to possess an increasing width the farther one progressed away from its protruding end. That is, the farther up inside the woman the shaft traveled, the wider the receiving orifice was forced open, so that with this sudden new depth of penetration Melody found her cuntal mouth stretched ever wider at the completion of each of these ever deepening thrusts.

Another adjustment was now made to the mechanism of the clock. At a word from Mlle. T. Alex moved the lever which controlled the flow of water, which powered the device, an additional two or three notches farther on the scale. There was a new, stronger rush of water through the ceiling and into the intake pipe of the contraption, and an instant later I heard and saw the huge machine kick into a much higher gear. The thrusting of the steel shaft within the depths of its female receptacle, which to this point had been at the same, slow, steady, consistent pace, became suddenly faster, plunging to and fro, in and out of the young woman with a much increased frequency.

Melody screamed out now at a higher pitch and frequency to match this new alteration in her ordeal. Her entire body shook in convulsive pleasure. For pleasure it certainly, ultimately was. Her second orgasm upon the padded table, under the ministrations of the water-clock, began almost immediately. Piercing, panicked cries turned into great, long, gasping intakes of breath, which then became extended timorous periods of silent shaking, as the blissful spasms of orgasm held the girl motionless and incapable of voicing her delight. And then would come at last the final choking, guttural scream of release.

Again and again this cycle of orgasmic rise and release was repeated with no sense that the energies or the passions of the young subject were flagging in the least.

Mlle. T. drew me aside, where her voice could be heard above the cries of the girl. She then spoke into my ear. "Melody will endure a total of three hours under the clock today." She indicated the huge wooden face of the clock above us, the hour and minute hands of which I had noted earlier to have been standing straight up at the "twelve o'clock" position. Now the minute hand had moved down to nearly twenty after the hour.

Obviously the clock-face was designed to display the length of time the machine was in continuous operation. Melody had over two-and-a-half hours yet to go.

Mlle. T. spoke again into my ear. "This will be our Melody's final session. She had done exceedingly well at her exercises and in a few days she will leave us for her new home. I believe her new master will find her most satisfactory."

I looked into the face of Mlle. T. and into the face of young Melody. The contrast of ultimate passion and ultimate serenity.

We remained there in the candle-lit chamber, witness to Melody's final ecstasies under the wooden face of the water-clock for nearly an hour longer.

Mlle. T. roused herself then, announced that it was well time for our lunch, and I followed her, rather reluctantly, out through the door and back down the winding passage, as the impassioned cries of Melody faded gradually in our wake.

CHAPTER EIGHT - THE WATERFALL

On the preceding evening, as you may remember, by way of the Chateau's "observation corridor", that magical hall of transparent mirrors - windows, opening onto the private lives of the school's inmates - I had had the opportunity of observing two of Mlle. T.'s younger charges, the virginal, though promiscuously-natured Ariel, and Jennifer, the timid friend to the former, both dark-haired angels of sixteen, as the two roommates engaged in lascivious play together in one of their chamber's single beds.

Mlle. T. had mentioned, as she stood at my elbow there on the shaded side of the glass, that, while the more aggressive of the two, the wickedly pleasurable Ariel was to have her promiscuity towards her sister females curbed by a mysteriously hinted at procedure which would take place in the very near future, the reticence of Ariel's partner, young Jennifer, where activities of a

sexual nature were concerned were to be dissuaded and her natural proclivities toward carnality enhanced by a likewise mysterious procedure to come.

On the evening following my introduction to the fascinating workings of the Chateau's amazing water-clock and the ecstasies that mere water pressure could provide a young female when creative modern technology and the directed willpower of Man were thoughtfully applied, Mlle. T. invited me to become witness to the manner in which a much simpler application of that same, simple, liquid element of nature could be utilized toward the purpose of turning the above-mentioned Jennifer from a shy, tentative creature into one for whom not even the most extreme excesses of sexual pleasure would adequately satisfy her soon to be whetted appetites.

The chamber into which Mlle. T. led me for the viewing of this procedure was, indeed, very much like that which had contained the apparatus of Alex's ingenious water-clock, as was not too surprising given that the principle element of the room's design came from the same watery spring that had powered the first. However, in the case at hand, the water flowed into this

particular chamber, not through the ceiling at the far end of the room, but rather from an opening at the room's very centre.

There, just under the ceiling at this point, and below the opening of a pipe connecting with the Chateau's nearby spring, had been fixed a sort of oblong tin basin of about five feet in length and about three feet in width. Down from this basin there dangled three long hoses of stiff India rubber, to each of which small graduated clamps had been attached a few inches from their ends. These hose ends, in turn, hung to a level of about a foot or so above the surface of a polished wooden table fixed to an immovable platform in the room's centre.

The purpose of the snakelike configuration of hoses above was unfathomable to me, but the design of the wooden table was clear from my observance of other such devices at the Mlle. T.'s school, for this table was fitted out with the same series of silver-buckled leather straps that by now I immediately recognized as being for the purpose of restraining the Chateau's young charges.

The redoubtable Alex was there when we arrived, his visage calm and emotionless as ever as he went about adjusting the stiff

hoses and their clamps with the loving care of the inventor for his invention. And a moment or two after myself and Mlle. T. had arrived, Karl entered the room as well, accompanied by the beautiful, though painfully timid young Jennifer.

She came without compunction, padding along behind the silent servant acquiescently enough in her bare feet, though her eyes were wide and wary, no doubt wondering what new "lesson" her harsh Mistress had planned for her.

I watched her approach. She met my gaze and I felt myself blush uncontrollably. After all, had I not observed this same young girl just the night before rolling blissfully in the arms of her wicked little roommate, Ariel? Had I not watched and listened as the girl had writhed and tossed under the delicious assault of her friend's busy tongue, until at last this same innocent-looking young nymph, as tender and fresh as any mythical denizen of some far off enchanted forest, had cried and screamed out her orgasmic pleasure, echoing the rich, full passion of her young womanhood again and again? Had I not seen this same girl's head of raven-dark hair bury itself between the even darker curls of her mischievous

companion, the virginal but promising Ariel, until she too was bucking and gurgling with equal pleasure?

And yet, it was still this impression of innocence that overcame all my intimate, though clandestine, knowledge of the girl and, as Karl assisted with the removal of the girl's short silk tunic and Jennifer's nakedness was unfolded once more unto my view, I confess I blushed like a bridegroom.

However it was not to me, but to the polished table before us that Jennifer was now to be wedded, and it was to the three down-hanging phalli above that the young "bride's" eyes were now drawn in clear incomprehension, the purpose of the apparatus still as much a mystery to her as it was to myself.

The girl was lifted onto the table and the hands of both Karl and Alex made quick work of securing the supple leather straps across the much more tender hide of the girl.

I must note here that the configuration of straps upon this particular table were, in fact, somewhat unique from others I had observed previously at the Chateau. There were about ten separate straps, as I recall, more than upon any like table I had seen before. First there were the usual straps restraining wrists

and ankles, the former fixing wrists tightly to the table, not with the girl's arms stretched high above her head as I had come to expect, but binding them immovably to the table at the girl's sides. There were, in addition, two straps binding the girl's upper arms tightly to the table as well. Jennifer's legs, widely spread, so that I could easily observe the delicate folds of the small, soft, girlish slit between, had been draped over the table's end, bending at the knees, so that her ankles could be strapped to the table legs below. Again, as in the case of her arms, an additional pair of straps crossed the girl's legs, just at mid-thigh, fixing both appendages in place as immovable as stone.

Now came the application of additional restraints. Two wide leather straps were drawn across the girl's torso, one just above, and the other just below, her small, tender-looking breasts, and were pulled tight, causing the twin, sweet pears to bulge upward more pronounced than was their want, the small, rose-coloured nipples ripening to impetuous points forcibly directed toward the ceiling above, from which dangled the India rubber hoses, their ends not six inches above those tender nubbins of flesh.

Yet another, wider, strap was now buckled across the girl's narrow waist, just above her hips, and when all was done at last, young Jennifer lay fixed to the smooth surface of the table so tightly and immovably that not even a violent earthquake would have moved her body out of position.

A small leather pillow was brought, and this was placed beneath Jennifer's head. All that remained to be done was to fix the usual hard rubber bit between the girl's fine, white teeth, and then all was truly ready.

It was then that Mlle. T. explained the "ordeal of the water" to me in full.

I have noted that two of the dangling hoses from the ceiling above now hung just a few inches above Jennifer's taut young nipples. The third of these hoses was now positioned about six inches or so above the sweet junction of the girl's widely splayed thighs, its end was now aimed, by Alex's knowing hand, directly at the small folds of flesh at the summit of Jennifer's slit, below which the girl's delicate clitoris lay hidden.

The Ordeal of the Water. I suppose my own innocence and naiveté must have been giving way as my education at the Chateau had progressed so far, for now, even as Mlle.

T. went about explaining the nature of the "ordeal", I had already begun to guess at it.

The procedure was perhaps the most simple, and yet the most ingenious of all the many operations I observed in my years at the Chateau Noir. It was as follows. Water from the neighbouring fresh-water spring was pumped through an opening in the chamber's ceiling and into the large collection pan a few inches below. From this collection pan there were suspended the three hoses fed by the water from above. The flow of that water through the stiff rubber hoses could then be regulated by way of the graduated clamps near the end of each of hose.

And finally, the water falling from the hose ends would, with a force and regularity that was adjustable by the fine degrees of the each hose's individual clamp, spill onto the tender flesh of the girl strapped immovably below. The three intended targets of the dripping water? The little red nipples at the summit of those twin pear-shaped breasts, and the small nub of the girl's sensitive clitoris.

The girl who lay strapped before us listened to Mlle. T.'s explanation as intently as did I, and as the purpose for the apparatus

above became clear to her, I saw her wriggle a bit against the confinement of her restraints, or attempt to wriggle, that is, for this slight testing of her bindings proved absolutely fruitless. Jennifer was held quite motionless, her tentative struggle amounting to results that were little more than a slight vibration of her small frame, a sort of shiver.

Indeed, there must have been in the girl's mind no real need for struggle. The "ordeal" she now understood herself about to induce surely must have seemed something much less uncomfortable than many other procedures she had no doubt heard rumoured, or even reported to her first hand, by her sister students. But for all that, the bit, the security of her restraints, all this must have yet given the girl pause to wonder if something more alarming perhaps lay ahead in the "ordeal of the water."

Mlle. T. now approached the head of the table, as I had seen her do before and have seen her do uncounted times since, in a brief, controlled expression of care and feeling for her young charges just before an important lesson or test in their training. She stood for a moment, stroking the girl's forehead, brushing away the straight, dark hair, mopping at the small glint of moisture the

warm dampness of the room or the girl's apprehensive excitement had precipitated.

"Now, my dear. This will test you more than you anticipate, I fear. And that is good. For what you are to learn here is the excitement of the flesh that you must not attempt to escape. It is the source of man's pleasure, and the source of a woman's power as well. That is the lesson of the Water. It is the pleasure that cannot be avoided, that should not be feared. It is the great truth that there is no degree of pleasure that a woman cannot endure. Once you accept this, once you experience this, you will never run from ecstasy again. You will seek it in the beds of men and women. You will not be able to live without it. It will become as necessary to the sustenance of your life as food, as air, as water itself. And throughout your life you will know no single pleasure as intense as the pleasure you are about to experience now."

I saw Mlle. T. smile indulgently at the obvious look of panic from the girl lying before her. "You will struggle, my dear. You will attempt to escape the caress of the water with all your heart and soul, so intense will be the pleasure it affords. But, after a time, you will transcend that pleasure, you

will overcome that panic, that fear. And you will be stronger for it, as are all my girls when their training has come to an end."

Mlle. T.'s brief smile had come and gone in an instant. "So be brave, my dear Jennifer," she called, stepping back from the table and motioning to Alex to set the "ordeal" in motion. A small, brave whimper came in answer from the bound girl, as Alex moved to the far wall, into which was set a small hand-crank. Two quick turns of this and there was a liquid rush of water into the reservoir pan just beneath the ceiling. The servant waited a moment or two, then backed the incoming current of water of slightly with one-and-a-half reverse turns of the crank. He then walked back to the restraining table and began to adjust the clamps fixed to the three rubber hoses.

Jennifer gasped through her gagging bit, as the first cool droplets of water fell from the end of the first hose and landed with a soft plop upon the tip of her straining left breast. The girl's eyes watched as the dripping became a steady plop... plop... plop against the little rosette nub. Her eyes darted right as a second stream of droplets opened onto her other breast as well. Her reactions were not of panic now, or of alarm. She

simply seemed to attune herself to the strange feel of this new sensation, collecting her impressions, absorbing the sensory input and apparently judging it to be easily endurable.

It was not until the adjusting clamp on the third hose, the one suspended above the tender apex of the girl's parted sex opening, that Jennifer seemed to have pause in her acceptance of her unusual circumstances. As the first few droplets pattered down upon the pink hood covering her sweet clit, the girl genuinely tried to wriggle away from this new watery stimulation, much as I had seen her attempt to squirm away from the first, tentative lapping of her roommate's little tongue the night before. But here, of course, there was no room to squirm away. So tightly was our Jennifer bound, as I have said, that not even the most violent undulation of her frame could have moved any of the three fleshy targets from the precise aim of the continuously falling spring water.

Adjusting to this additional stimulus to her lower regions, as I say, appeared to be somewhat more difficult for Jennifer to reconcile herself to. Her eyes now held more than a note of panic. It was the

voluptuous tickle of water against the top of her slit that was torturing her now, the sensation having not as of yet been converted into a sensuality of a more sexual nature.

Such a conversion was not more than a few minutes in developing however, as Mlle. T. attracted silently my notice to a small, physical change in the girl. As I watched, I witnessed the change at the moment it occurred. The droplets of water upon Jennifer's young nipples had caused those red nubbins to grow almost instantly stiff and erect, the natural result of the cool temperature of the water falling against warm flesh. Such a reaction would have occurred in a cool bath or a brisk northern breeze. There was nothing at all sexual about it.

But now, again, as I stood witness, the falling water from the third hose, the one directed to the girl's parted sex, was having an effect that could only have been one of true arousal. Slowly, as if by degrees in strict accord to the number of droplets as they fell upon the hood of flesh above, Jennifer's young clitoris began to put forth an appearance from beneath that hood. Soon it stood proudly, and hugely for such a small

young woman, all a glowing pink, a little nub, like a large pink pearl, pulsing with every new droplet of water that fell.

Jennifer, while perhaps not aware in her innocence the physical manifestation her arousal presented us, was most certainly aware of the emotional reactions bubbling sweetly within her at the watery stimulation of her young clit. She had begun to breath pantingly around the gag of her rubber bit. There was a more definite sheen of perspiration upon her soft brow. Indeed, her entire body was covered by this sheen of newly aroused passion.

No doubt her body would by now have been tossing and writhing with great abandon had her binding restraints not prevented any such motion. As if was, only a trembling, a violent tightening and releasing of young muscle in coltish legs, arms and heaving torso alike announced the sensations coursing through a body coming suddenly, reluctantly, alive with lust.

I was about to direct a question to Mlle. T., who stood at my shoulder, as to how long the girl's torment was prescribed to endure, when a new sound from Jennifer silenced me.

"Guh... guh... gawwwww...!"

She seemed to be experiencing some difficulty in breathing around the obstruction of her rubber bit. There was then a massively drawn intake of breath, followed by a sort of muscular convulsion throughout her entire body, retrained to a mere protracted tremor beneath the tight leather straps.

Then, a scream as from the depths of hell itself caused me to jump back in alarm.

Mlle. T.'s whispered at my side. "Now it has started, Thomas. And so soon!"

A cry begun as a gagging, choked intake of breath was followed by a two-note shrieking wail, as if of unendurable torment. The cry echoed through the chamber again and again, blending into new cries from their original source. The young girl's orgasms must have been intense beyond anything one could imagine.

Much later, when my knowledge of the Chateau Noir and the methods of its mistress had grown, Mlle. T. told me that it, indeed, was the opinion of many experts the world over and the testimony of many an ancient text down through the ages that the pleasures of orgasm for the woman, when property precipitated, are of an intensity completely unachievable by the male of the species.

My observation of young Jennifer, as she glided from one high summit of orgasmic response to the next under the Ordeal of the Water bore this out with impunity. And I will go further, and say that I believe to this very day that no male would be able to endure such intensity of pleasure without losing his life or, at least, his sanity. And it is this, I believe, this incapacity to experience the apex of human pleasure, that apex reserved exclusively for the female, that ultimately accounts for the male's primordial fascination with the female orgasm, the fear of it, and that based in jealousy of course, which often leads to the baser compulsion to dominate the female and, in more purer male souls, to a heart-felt reverence for the ultimate sacredness of the female that is the just basis for her clear superiority over the male.

So it was that, without quite knowing it then, I was this day becoming a giant step closer to discovering the deeply underlying philosophy, the basic underpinning as it were, of the Chateau Noir and all that occurred there.

As for young Jennifer? Her ordeal lasted over two entire days and two entire nights! Sometime during the closing hours Mlle. T.

and myself visited that chamber once again. By this time the girl seemed barely sane. Her voice had long hours since grown hoarse from her prolonged screams of orgasmic release, and now each of Jennifer's successive peaks of passion was accompanied by only a harsh whispery exhalation of breath around the lubricated bit between her tightly clenched teeth.

Likewise had the soft leather restraints which still held her so tightly bound been carefully lubricated to prevent chafing through the long hours of desperate struggle for release and the convulsive spasms of pleasure attained.

Jennifer's hollow eyes stared straight ahead now, except for when the clenched tightly shut against each on-coming wave of passion. The timbers of the wooden table creaked and groaned as each of these waves swept across the young woman held bound to them, so strenuous were her muscular tugs and strainings against the leather straps.

At the conclusion of each of these spasms, a fresh trickle of drool would escape from the sweet, bitted mouth, and fresh beads of sweet-scented perspiration, the dew of female orgasm, would blossom along the length of Jennifer's tensed, naked flesh.

The water from the three torturingly pleasuring hoses ran steadily across the table's waxed surface to run away into a collecting earthenware vessel placed unto the floor beneath, a sweet mixture of fresh spring water with the luxuriant, perfumed effluvia of a beautiful young woman undergoing the absolute ultimate in earthly pleasure.

What a sweet libation such liquid would make!

Not surprisingly, Mlle. T. was well aware of this truth, as indeed the woman seemed aware of all great truths. The sweet liquid in the jar below the table was to be bottled at the Chateau Noir and sold, at quite an exorbitant price naturally, to one or two of Mlle. T.'s most affluent customers.

CHAPTER NINE - NIGHT OBSERVATIONS

Not many nights later, Mlle. T. once again invited me into the "observation corridor" of the Chateau Noir, in order to view again a few of her charges in their most private moments. It was late in the evening as it happened, just an hour or so before midnight. Mlle. T. again lit our way along the dark corridor with a single lighted candle held aloft before us.

This time it was a completely different range of hallways into which the Mistress drew me. Black velvet tapestries lined the walls of the narrow passage as before, and similar material covered the oaken floorboards, the combination serving to insulate the rooms the corridor followed from any sound that we, the hidden observers, might make. Here the same large, gold framed "windows" - the Chateau's ingenious two-way mirrors - looked in on chambers within the building that I had not heretofore seen or visited.

"This is our Bathing Chamber," said Mlle. T., again as before, assuming the role of tour guide. "I believe we have arrived too late for our Ariel's bath, but no matter, we will see her again later on."

I looked to the Mistress for further explanation, but her perfunctory nod, directing my gaze back towards the window, silenced any inquiry.

Indeed, we did seemed to have missed seeing young Ariel at her bath. The raven-curled sixteen-year-old was already stepping from a large, deep, rock-lined pool of steamy, bubbling water, which had been constructed below the level of the floor of the large room.

This waters of this bathing chamber were heated to a comfortably fevered temperature, I was told, my a natural underground spring, the sultry twin of that cool-water spring which the resourceful Alex had employed to drive his water-clock.

"The temperature of this spring is quite hot throughout the year," said Mlle. T. "The soothing heat and natural effervescence of the water is quite therapeutic."

The girls at the Chateau were bathed here once each day, the newer girls, like

Ariel, at the attentive hands of some of the older students.

Having stepped from the bubbling water, this same Ariel now stood nakedly exposed before our hidden eyes in all her tantalizing young beauty. She could have been some delicate young faun, pausing by a misty, still pond, caught by moonlight and captured upon canvas by one of our more Romantic painters, her skin all aglow from the warm light of the many candles which illuminated the room.

Ariel's enticing nakedness was quickly concealed from our view by huge towels wielded by two of Mlle. T.'s older girls dressed in the customary brief, white silk tunics. The hands of these two busied themselves vigorously in rubbing the soft, heat-moistened flesh of their younger sister until she flushed and glowed even warmer in the candlelight.

A third attendant approached as the drying of the girl was completed, this girl baring a tray that held several crystal jars of various interesting and exotic shapes. The towels were now withdrawn from the Ariel's form, revealing her, naked once again, before our welcoming eyes. The first two attendants assisted the younger girl from a

standing position into a bending stance across the back of a wooden chair which stood nearby.

Bent low at the waist and facing away from our viewing window, Ariel unknowingly presented to us her bare backside and the delicious secrets for the moment concealed between the apple cheeks of that fine, taut bottom.

Firm, feminine hands drew the girl's knees gently apart. What a glorious sight was then revealed! A small, narrow-lined slit of pink, nestled within the dividing crevice of her up-turned behind, crowned by the tiny aperture of her girlish nether hole. Tiny curls of darkness, glistening with moisture where the fluffy towels had failed to venture, surrounded this garden of delight, making the sight a pure tantalization of the senses.

From the corner of my eye, I noticed Mlle. T. quietly observing my reactions, and I struggled silently to maintain at least an appearance of propriety under the stimulation of what I was observing.

I should perhaps mention here that my senses by this time, but a few short days into my first visit at the Chateau Noir, had indeed been undergoing a gradual quickening unlike

any I had known in my life previously. True, I had at my young age experienced the normal urges and desires of my sex, the secret, midnight yearnings toward release that all young men know and grapple with daily.

But now, as each day, as each hour, at the Chateau Noir passed slowly by, I felt these dark desires and impulses from the erotic side of my nature slowly growing, as if with each new sight and sensation the Chateau presented before my view a seed had been planted, and the vegetation now sprouting up from that fertilization was being carefully tended and cultivated by the dark spirit of Chateau itself.

I focused my gaze more intently upon the activities beyond the mirrored glass before me, trying to suppress any outward show of the emotions I was experiencing.

The two attendants were now engaged in perfuming the secret flowers of young Ariel's exposed backside. Thin glass wands were withdrawn from two of the oddly shaped crystal vessels, one containing a fluid of dark red and the other a light, golden amber. The girl seemed to start and tremble at the first touch of the small glass rods to her bare flesh. The two older girls

murmured calming reassurances as the glass traced thin lines of perfumed wetness along the pinkness of the girl's young sex, the lips of which seemed to contract under the cold sting, this, I assumed, from the alcohol contained in the exotic mixtures.

I thought I heard a slight whimper of discomfort from Ariel, as one of the glass rods entered presumptuously into the area of her tiny nether hole. The attendant applying the perfume to this area seemed to hesitate there, as if reluctant to withdraw to other, less forbidden precincts, the tip of the glass wand tracing wetly all around the tight opening, and then, just as I expected it to move away as the entire area surrounding the little aperture had been thoroughly wetted by the perfume, the attendant's wrist suddenly moved to send the tip of the glass applicator fully two inches into the channel of that aperture.

Ariel gasped loudly at the unexpected intrusion, nearly bucking up from her trembling stance over the chair. The third female attendant had, however, a few moments before set down her tray of crystal jars, and had positioned herself to quickly catch the younger girl about the waist and hold her firmly should just such a reaction

take place. This young woman strongly wrestled the younger girl against the chair back, holding her with strong arms until the undoubtedly intense internal burning of the perfume had somewhat subsided.

The two perfuming attendants continued with their duties undaunted, until their work was complete. The glass wands were withdrawn, including the one that had been slipped up Ariel's young backside. I confess I was somewhat disappointed that one of the rods had not ventured into the channel of the girl's sex as well, but it was apparently not to be. My lascivious and voyeuristic desires were soon to be gratified in a nearly similar manner, however, as Ariel's position was now rearranged upon the smooth wooden chair.

A moment later, Ariel was seated upon the chair she had been bent across. One of her attendants stood behind the chair back, while the remaining two knelt between Ariel's widely splayed thighs. Apparently the young girl was now to be rewarded for her patience and endurance, for the two crouching young women began to offer gentle caresses to the smooth flesh of the girl's inner thighs, while their sister above

commenced to soothingly massage Ariel's graceful neck and shoulders.

Ariel's sweet eyes fluttered closed as the combined caresses began to relax her. Her shoulder muscles became slack, warm clay to the student sculpting her from above. But Ariel's relaxation became altered somewhat as the caresses from below ventured ever closer to the apex of her coltish thighs. The gentle, feminine fingers stroked along these delicate inner surfaces, in and back, in and back, sliding with each inward, tickling stroke nearer and still nearer to the pink flower that lay waiting. The soft, pink petals of that young flower had now become slightly swollen in delicious anticipation of what was to come, and when the fingers at last reached their destination, the girl erupted in her sat with an instantaneous climax that wetted the faces of both kneeling attendants.

"Aghhhhhhhhh!" The kneeling pair welcomed the warm rain of their subject's orgasmic response quite eagerly, and dipped forward their heads to offer duel tongues to the source of that sweet stream of moisture.

Ariel felt the attack of the twin tongues and again bucked upwards powerfully in the chair, but the firm hands of the attendant above quickly restrained her with a gentle

downward pressure upon the girl's shoulders, forcing Ariel to keep her seat and endure the fierce onslaught of her pleasure.

"Ghuhhh... Haaaaaaaaaaaa!" Female fingers now joined female tongues as the two attendants attempted skillfully to prolong the pleasures their younger sister was experiencing. For some minutes the orgasmic surges within Ariel's small frame rolled on, and still onwards. The girl seemed capable of climbing the very walls in her explosive excitement, had she not been adequately restrained by her sister above. Her eyes flashed open widely again and again, only to clench violently shut as each successive wave of intense pleasure came crashing over her young body.

There was a virtual lake between the legs of the young girl now, and the two kneeling attendants seemed to struggle valiantly to catch every renewed spurt at its source, not wanting to miss an ounce of the precious fluid.

Another series of sharp cries.

Again and again, did the seated young girl writhe up in her seat to cry out with another, and yet another peak of girlish passion, until it seemed that such a small body could not possibly contain such

pleasure. It must have been so, for with one, final upward surge, which forced the young girl nearly from the restraining grip of her attendant above, Ariel was suddenly convulsed and racked with a quaking and inward churning surpassing all those that had gone before. She strained and stretched upwards into a near standing position above the chair, her two kneeling sisters rising along with her in order to maintain their teasing contact within the valley of the girl's sex. There was one, final, heart-rending shriek.

A screaming wail of heart-breaking note and intensity. The cry trailed off after several long seconds, coming to a end in a soft, tearful whine, as Ariel fell back into her chair, her overwrought young body collapsing into unconsciousness.

We watched, Mlle. T. and I, as the insensible Ariel was carried from the steam-shrouded bathing room by her three attendants.

"Young Ariel's night of pleasure has just begun," said Mlle. T., again watching my now breathless excitement at what I had just witnessed. She turned away, however, before I could meet her glance. "Her three sisters students will pleasure her again in her

own chamber. So intense and exhausting will be her lesbian delights this night that ammonia will be used on more than one occasion to bring her up from unconsciousness. I have given strict orders that between now and midnight, our Ariel is to have to respite whatsoever.

"For you see," said Mlle. T., this time meeting my inquisitive gaze, "this is to be young Ariel's final night of passion, at least of the passions she has heretofore known: the pleasures of other girls and the more secret delights of her own fingers between her legs. Tomorrow, all those familiar pleasures will be beyond her. As you will see, come midnight."

My eyes displayed my complete lack of comprehension. "You will recall that I said our Ariel had passions that must be curbed?" said Mlle. T. "That Ariel has been destined to become the companion of a certain individual, an Arab gentleman, who insists that she be open to the sexual enjoyment of men only, and so not inclined to the pleasures of other girls or of herself even, through solitary masturbation?"

I nodded, remembering. "Well, tonight, Thomas," she continued, "you will witness the curbing of those passions in our Ariel

forever. After tonight, only a man will be able to please her, and only in a certain very specific way."

Of course, I did not understand. But I knew by now not to inquire of Mlle. T. what she would not willingly reveal. The Mistress of the Chateau Noir would not be rushed.

I checked my watch. Midnight was but an hour away.

CHAPTER TEN - OBSERVATIONS CONTINUED

I spent the remaining hour before my second midnight appointment in Mlle. T.'s bed chamber wandering alone along that velvet-lined corridor of transparent mirrors, pausing here and there to gaze through several of the portholes onto the various scenes beyond.

Here were two of the Chateau's younger students, one dark, one light, both blissfully entwined in one other's arms, squirming anxiously head-to-tail in a girlish wrestle, each no doubt seeking to surpass the other in the pleasures she was affording her sister. I wondered for a moment whether the activities in this case had been proscribed by their Mistress, or whether the two were engaged in affections that had been forbidden them, and so were accruing punishments to become due later on. Punishments that I might be witness to.

Another shaded window looked into the bed chamber of little Beverly, whose

smallish form I recognized instantly from her short, bright, blonde hair above, and her complete lack of it below. This was the same girl I had seen "plucked" on my first invited visit to the Mlle.'s bed chamber.

The young girl lay upon her narrow bed now, both hands clutched between her fine, coltish thighs, rubbing and teasing herself insistently, just as Mlle. T. had predicted she would, the systematic removal of her fine pubic curls having stimulated the girl to a state of near constant arousal.

Indeed, the girl showed much evidence of the long hours she had spent at this secret self-play since her midnight operation. Her strong inner thighs looked somewhat bruised below the wetness there, and there were unmistakable dark circles beneath the girl's eyes that held told a tale of several days lack of sleep.

Later I would mention this to Mlle. T., who would then explain that the girl might be sedated should her youthful endurance of such over-extended periods of pleasuring prove detrimental to her health.

Several windows further down the corridor I came upon a view of a room I had seen once before. It was that occupied my Allison, the solitary masturbator Mlle. T.

had shown me through this same corridor window earlier. Though wild with passion then, the curly-haired brunette now appeared most calm and angelic in sleep. Careful observation of the exposed curls peeking from under the hem of her white tunic, however, clearly demonstrated that this was only a temporary pause in Allison's secret activity, for the slight foliage there was as wet with recent excitement as had been the bare pubice of young Beverly.

At the base of Allison's "window" in the corridor I now noticed two small plaques had been hung by little loops of golden chain, draped over a nail. The plaques had been cut from thin sheets of wood, painted black, and lettered with the following two legends: "THE POLE" and "THE BRAND."

My brow furrowed as I wondered what these pronouncements might signify, but could come to no certain conclusion.

Further still along the corridor, I found the window into the chamber assigned to young Stephanie. This was, I remembered, the girl I had seen on that earlier occasion as well lying restrained in her bed, forcibly forbidden the pleasures of her own fingers until some later date.

The brown-haired girl still lay restrained as she had been then, some days before, but this time there were a few changes. Stephanie's position had been changed. She had been pulled down the bed until her small behind rested right at the mattress edge, her legs hanging over its far end and strapped into place against the bed's iron legs.

Something else was different as well. A most singular-looking device of some kind had been placed upon a cart, which had then been wheeled into place between the girl's parted thighs. This device, I quickly realized, must be "the Tongue" which I had heard Mlle. T. mysteriously allude to.

It consisted of an unfathomable configuration of clock-work, no doubt designed my the ingenious Alex, maker of the Chateau's water-clock, as well as many other clever devices I was to see as my stay at the Chateau drew on. This particular device appeared to be powered by an inner spring that could be wound up and left to run unattended, for there was no one in the room but Stephanie.

The purpose of the device was clear. At the centre of a conglomeration of churning and ticking gears there was a two-foot length of soft leather, about two inches in width,

which flew through the air in a continuous circular arc, bound to a central flywheel of the device.

The remarkable gadget had been placed close enough up between Stephanie's splayed thighs so that each whirring cycle of the clock-work send that strip of soft leather - that "Tongue" - smacking down with some considerable force into the exposed centre of the girl's defenseless vulva.

I say the "Tongue" whipped into the girl's sex with some force, but it was apparent that that force had been carefully regulated so as to cause no serious damage to Stephanie's delicate membranes, but to deliver quite a stinging blow there nevertheless.

There was no sound from beyond the glass. I gathered that this must have been one of the Chateau's soundproof chambers. However, had I been able to listen to the sounds within, no doubt I would have heard the most alarming shrieks from the girl within.

Stephanie's eyes were wilder than they had been at the orgasmic moment when she had failed to withstand the "test" of her Mistress's stimulation, which I had witnessed upon the first day of my arrival at

the Chateau, and which I have described earlier in these pages.

The girl's arms and legs struggled with a fierceness remarkable for one of such tender age, the straps that held her arms stretched back along the bed pulled to the tautness of bowstrings.

But no amount of wild resistance would do the girl a bit of good. The straps held her fast. She could but raise her unbound midsection upwards from the mattress, but that would only bring the stinging lash of the "tongue" down upon the full length of her girlish slit, instead of upon the uppermost portion near her clit alone, and so no respite was to be gained at all through that.

How long had the girl's punishment gone on? How long might it yet continue? To these questions I had no answer. I looked on for a few more minutes there, and then left the silently screaming girl, to continue on down the corridor in search of another particular window.

Finally, I came upon the shadowed mirror that looked into the chamber of sixteen-year-old Ariel. The dark-haired virgin was seated upon a wooden straight-backed chair at her beside, just a few inches beyond the glass through which I gazed.

She appeared worried, her head down, the curling bangs of her sweet dark hair nearly obscuring my view of her eyes.

She seemed to be struggling with some troubling thought or other, her hands gripped tightly upon her knees. Suddenly she threw back her head and gave a little whimper of frustration. Her eyes now revealed from behind the dark curtain of her hair were feverish with emotion, though with what specific emotion I could not as yet determine.

The answer became apparent in the next moment, as the young girl seemed to come to some decision, released her knees, the tight grip of her hands there leaving the dark remnants of a slight bruising, and slid those hands instead quickly up along her thighs to their sweet junction, veiled by the hem of her short silk tunic.

Ariel had been attempting to restrain herself from touching the area her hands were so avidly exploring now, possibly following a prohibition from her Mistress. But now her resolve was scattered to the winds, as she obviously worked diligently to bring herself off as quickly as possible.

The girl's effort was to prove all in vain, however, for the next instant the door to the

chamber flew wide open. It was the servant, Karl. Without preamble, he lifted the girl bodily from her chair and carried her from the room, the door swinging closed to latch behind him.

I quickly dug my watch from my pocket. Yes, it was ten minutes 'til midnight. Ariel had an appointment with Mlle. T.

And so did I.

I hurried back down the corridor toward the stairway, but before I did so, I turned back to the window I had just looking through, and noticed for the first time the little plaque which dangled from the lower frame. It read: "THE PLUCKING."

I thought for a moment of the plaques I had seen earlier, and then hurried on my way.

CHAPTER ELEVEN - ARIEL

The clock on the mantelpiece above the fireplace in Mlle. T.'s bed chamber was just striking midnight as I rushed breathlessly into the room. Mlle. T. was there, along with the servant, Karl, and one other. The mysterious Jo Lin, she of the exotic oriental beauty and sure knowledge of many ancient and forbidden practices, was present as well. She was dressed in silk robe, a kimono, of the blackest silk I had ever seen. There seemed to be a slice of midnight in that dark garment, and the glowing firelight, and the many lighted candles which also burned within the room, scattered an ever changing, ever flowing, field of stars across its curving contours.

Young Ariel had already been placed and bound in position on her back along an oddly-shaped table, upholstered in dark leather. This unusual piece of furniture had been constructed in the shape of a horizontal "Y", consisting of a main section about three feet wide, branching out in opposite angles

into two narrower wings, each about seven inches in width, at one end.

The manner in which the young student had been strapped onto this table made the idea behind its strange design very clear. Ariel lay with her back against the wider section, that being the head of the ottoman, and wide her legs bound to the two off-shooting wings at its foot, so that her body was positioned to form the "Y" as well. The angle of her widely parted thighs matched the angle of the table's wings, so that Ariel lay naked now, with her open, virginal sex exposed to the view of all in the flickering light of the log fire. Open indeed, for apparently Ariel had been carefully shaved of the dark, downy moss that had until recently grown there.

The usual silver-buckled leather straps bound the girl in her place, arms stretched high over her head, waist held securely against the leather-padded table, and each leg was wrapped in a circling spiral of straps which kept them absolutely immovable against their padded supports.

Such configurations of straps I had by now, of course, seen many times on other of the Chateau's students, but there was one unusual addition in the case of young Ariel.

Instead of the rubber bit I had become accustomed to seeing used alone, which, as Mlle. T. had described, would leave a girl free to orally express her discomfort or her excitement, while at the same time reducing the danger of any unintentional self-inflicted damage to her teeth or tongue, the mouth of young Ariel, once bitted as usual, had also been swathed in a white bandage, circling her head in many turns until it the girl's mouth had been wrapped to a thickness that would undoubtedly preclude her emitting even the slightest sound.

This baffled me, as Mlle. T. had expressed to me the importance of hearing her girls' cries of passion, or of torment, as one means of judging the degree of the severity of those emotions. Here, however, it was apparent that Ariel was to be allowed to make no noise at all, except for the huffing of air through her unobstructed nostrils.

All this I took in within a second, as I entered the chamber. Mlle. T., having noted my abrupt arrival with a tight, but indulgent smile, nodded to Jo Lin that whatever ceremony was to take place here could now begin.

Jo Lin glided across the floor, and paused to stand before the dark and silent manservant Karl. A slight shift of her shoulders somehow released the black kimono, which fell into Karl's waiting hands, leaving the dark-haired oriental naked and beautiful in the firelight.

A hint of some enticing fragrance drifted to me from Jo Lin's uncovered form, a delicious scent which told eloquently and temptingly of dusty, far away lands. The woman moved around with measured, graceful step to face the reclining Ariel, who lay, as I have described, spread-eagle before the open hearth.

The woman looked for a moment into the eyes of the young girl bound before her. There was fear there, although I later learned that Ariel had been informed about what was about to occur, and had fully assented to the procedure I was here to witness. Still, there was a look of threatening panic in the girl's dark eyes.

Jo Lin must have seen the girl's apprehension as well, for she moved now to soothe that emotion. Delicate fingers stretched forth into the sweet apex of the straining "v" formed my the girl's narrow thighs. The touch of a single long-nailed

fingertip to the tender hood of the girl's clitoris, sent a ripple of sensation upwards and outward along Ariel's young body, raising a pattern of goose flesh from inner thighs to flat, taut stomach to cherry-tipped breasts. Both the bud of the girl's little clit and the twin nubs of her breasts were almost instantly erect and straining, wanting the caresses of the oriental beauty to continue.

Jo Lin now knelt down, her face just above the level of the girl's open sex. The knowing attentions of the woman were having the desired effect upon young Ariel. There appeared now a faint trace of moisture at the pink aperture at the base of the girl's slit, and the smooth-muscled plain of her belly was stirred by the flutter of arousal.

The huffing of air in and out through Ariel's nose became more noisome, as the fingers of Jo Lin continued to trace a teasing, soothing path up and down in the delicate furrow, stopping now and again at the top to flick for a moment or two against the tight bud of the girl's clit. The sounds of her rough breathing became also intermingled with small, faint moaning sounds from deep within the girl's throat that no gag or bandage would muffle.

I watched as the colour of the flesh bordering Ariel's delicate sex began to change subtly, the faint pink conch-colour deepening into a darker shade of red, the lips parting there as well to emit a thin trickle of wetness that lubricated the steadily stroking fingertips of Jo Lin's right hand.

It was the left hand of the older woman that now attracted my attention, however, as I noticed it reaching slowly downward in the direction of the floor. It searched for a moment just beneath the curtained underside of the table's end, found what it sought, and returned from beneath the curtain with a small rosewood casket. There were many intricate designs upon this small box, a few of which I recognized as script in what I believed to be Arabic.

Jo Lin, without pausing in her caressing of the increasingly excited young Ariel, sat the box upon the floor between her knees and silently opened the hinged lid. Silver light seemed to gleam from within, and the flickering firelight reflected off of several objects of glittering silver.

I felt a hand upon my shoulder, and Mlle. T.'s arm guided me into a better position to view what was about to occur. We soon stood side by side just behind the

kneeling Jo Lin and the spread-eagle Ariel, and slightly to one side, so that the light from the fireplace would now be blocked in its illumination of the young girl's exposed sex.

Mlle. T. leaned in close to my ear to whisper, "You will remember, Thomas, that I mentioned earlier that young Ariel's tendency to enjoy the caresses of other women and at her own hands was unacceptable to the master for whom she is intended?" I nodded, my mind full of suspicions and conjectures as to what the word, "PRUNING," lettered upon the small plaque I had seen hanging beneath Ariel's mirror/window might signify. Was this what I was about to learn?

"After tonight," continued Mlle. T., her voice still in a whisper, so as not to distract the two women before us, "our Ariel will be unable to enjoy such caresses, and will be able to find erotic relief only under the attentions of her intended male lover."

I moved my head slightly in a manner that indicated my failure to comprehend, but froze when I saw the fingers of Jo Lin's left hand remove one of the glittering silver items from within the rosewood box

between her knees, and knew instantly what that object was. A razor.

The resonance consisted of a long, intricately carved silver handle, fixed to a small crescent-shaped metal blade measuring but an inch from horn to horn. I could easily see that this blade was exceedingly sharp.

Now I knew, even without the further explanation that came from Mlle. T., the full truth and nature of what was about to occur. A "pruning." Ariel was to be deprived of those delicate, sweet toys that she was so adept at employing for her own private enjoyment of her young femininity, and that made her susceptible to the girlish caresses of her sister students.

It was true. Mlle. T. confirmed it so, quietly, before moving apart from where I stood to dissuade any further questioning upon my part. Left with no means of relieving her own natural feminine desires, either on her own or in the company of others of her own sex, young Ariel would necessarily turn her attentions toward her male master, finding her pleasure there where she had sought it elsewhere throughout her youth.

My emotions were a turmoil of wonder and, I must admit, arousal, as well as a heartfelt pity for the young woman who lay before me, rippling and squirming within her bonds as Jo Lin's caresses neared their inevitable conclusion. Though Mlle. T. assured me, then and later, that the pleasures young Ariel would experience in her new, altered, life would exceed by many expanses the joy she had know previously, I still thought it a hard cost for the girl, or any girl, to bare. I did, however, see flashing upon my mind a sudden vision of Ariel, her dark curls tossing, her body upheaving, her legs scrambling to hold onto the hips of her future male lover, his rampant member plunging again and again into the girl's sex to its very depths, as her screams of unimaginable pleasure rose higher and higher as deliriums of pleasure rose within her.

A sudden upward increase in the huffing breath through Ariel's widely flaring nostrils drew me back to what was occurring before me. The knowing hands of Jo Lin were about to bring the girl she attended to a crisis, the final rushing orgasm she would know under the caresses of any woman, her own self included.

Breath whistling now in its intensity, Ariel froze, straining against the leather straps, as the first crashing wave of her climax rocked her from head to toe. A whining, keening cry from beneath the her gag and mouth bandage accompanied the release of this first wave, as Ariel began her way convulsingly downward from her high summit of delight.

"Hmmmmmmmmmmmmmmm," the girl moaned contentedly beneath her gag.

I had glanced upward into Ariel's partially masked face at that moment, and saw her already wide eyes suddenly fly open even wider, her whine of joy suddenly replaced by a gurgling eruption of pure panic.

"Guh... Gahhhhhhhhhhhhhhhhhhhhh!"

I glanced instantly back towards the gaping juncture of the girl's thighs, and readily saw the reason for Ariel's abrupt alteration of emotion. Jo Lin had skillfully chosen the moment before, the instant that young Ariel had been descending from the throws of her orgasm, to make the initial necessary incision into the girl's delicate girl-flesh.

What followed was nearly a full minute or writhing and bucking and high, shrill

keening that no gag or muffling mouth bandage could restrain, as the practiced, knowing hands of Jo Lin went about her careful, neat trimming of Ariel's intimate pinkness. Throughout the hardest parts of the ordeal, Mlle. T. stood near the head of the table, holding her charges face between her hands, whispering soothingly to the girl, and applying cool, damp clothes to the girl's fevered young brow.

One particularly crucial slice, this at the very top of the girl's sex, sent Ariel, with a final, muffled shriek, suddenly downward into blissful unconsciousness. There remained but a few, neatening touches, and the work was soon complete.

Jo Lin replaced her bright razors in their rosewood casket and, having draped Ariel's weary loins with a red silk cloth, glided emotionlessly from the room, pausing only to accept upon her calm shoulders the silken folds of her midnight black kimono, placed there as she passed by the ever- attendant Karl.

CHAPTER TWELVE - ALLISON

Several days later, I was invited by Mlle. T. to attend her at another of the Chateau's training sessions. Once again, it was to be seventeen-year-old Allison to whom this session was dedicated, she of the haughty, superior air. The proud, unshakable girl who, for all her cool aloofness when in the company of her superiors, was the same girl I had watched entertain herself upon her own fingers in the supposed privacy of her bed chamber.

Young Allison was to be "broken" of her feigned disinterest in matters sexual by what Mlle. T. described as "a long and quite arduous series of procedures designed to reveal to the girl her true erotic nature." Today's event, however, was to be more of a demonstration, for my benefit more than for the benefit of the girl, herself. Mlle. T. explained that she intended to show me the 'natural, feminine heat lurking just below the girl's carefully controlled exterior facade.' "Beneath Allison's mask of disdain for the

erotic," said Mlle. T. "our Allison is quite the little wildcat. And though she remains a virgin, her inner drives are tearing the girl apart. These drives must be aroused to the point where she is no longer capable of denying them, to herself or to the world."

Allison apparently was not only a virgin where men were concerned, but she also remained innocent of the caresses of her sister females. And it was the natural, inborn tendency toward female-to-female lesbian intimacy that Mlle. T. proposed to demonstrate. The experiment took place in the dining room of the Chateau, just after the mid-day meal. The table had been cleared - the same heavy oaken dining table I have already described - and young Allison was brought in by the servant, Karl, accompanied by two of Mlle. T.'s students that I did not remember having seen before. They were two lush blondes of about eighteen. Twin sets of sparkling blue eyes looked openly and boldly into my own as the two girls entered. From the relaxed, casual attitude of the two, I took it that these must be of the Chateau's senior class, if not actual graduates. Mlle. T. later confirmed my assumptions. They were, indeed, very near their graduation dates, and would soon be

shipping off for the orient, the two contracted as a pair to one of the Chateau's leading sponsors.

The two blondes came to stand quietly near the wall opposite where I and Mlle. T. sat waiting. Allison looked from the two older girls to her Mistress, obviously wondering what was about to occur. Mlle. T. lead over to whisper, so that the others in the room could not hear.

"Watch," she said.

She then rose and approached her dark-haired charge, who stood apprehensively awaiting her Mistress's command. "Remove your tunic, my dear," said Mlle. T., perfunctorily. There was but a barely perceptible hesitation on Allison's part as she did as she was told. The wispy silken garment was shrugged from her shoulders, and it fell with a hushed rustle into a snowy puddle about the girl's feet. Then Allison stood motionless again, waiting for what might happen next. I have described young Allison earlier. Beautifully framed, her breasts proudly standing upon her out-thrust chest, the pink nipples small and erect, now, from their sudden exposure to the cool air of the room. Short, curly hair, the colour of rich, well-oiled mahogany crowned her

sweet head. A swatch of the same colour showed at the junction of her well-muscled thighs, which she now pressed modestly together as she stood. All in all, the girl was quite as beautiful as any of the girls I had seen at the Chateau, or anywhere else in my young life, for that matter. "Now," continued Mlle. T., once her charge had disrobed. "Stand and face your sisters, my dear." Allison looked to her Mistress in confusion, but then understood that she was referring to the two blondes standing across the table from her. She did as she was told, and stood facing the two.

"Ladies," said Mlle. T.

This apparently was sufficient instruction for the two young blondes, for they instantly cast off their own white silk tunics, casually tossing them aside, exposing two more of the most magnificently beautiful creatures I had ever seen. It was clear that their Mistress had discussed her plans for this event with the two in advance, for most of what came after this point occurred with very little direct instruction from their instructress. It was equally clear that young Allison had not idea at all as to what was afoot. The girl stood there, her eyes directed toward her two schoolmates,

nervously waiting for Mlle. T.'s next command. It came soon enough.

"Allison, I wish you to look at your two sisters here." said Mlle. T., approaching the young girl. "They are beautiful, are they not?" Allison did not reply at once. There was more than a degree of hesitation before she mumbled, uncertainly, "Y... yes, Mistress."

"Quite beautiful, wouldn't you say?" Mlle. T. asked.

"Y... yes, Mistress."

"Then say it, Allison!" Mlle. T. demanded, sharply of the girl. Allison swallowed audibly.

"Y... yes, Mistress. They are... they are... beautiful... Mistress."

Mlle. T. smiled, coolly. "That is fine, Allison," she said. "And since they are so beautiful," the woman continued. "No doubt you would consent to make love to the two of them, yes?" Allison's eyes widened in shock.

"N... no, Mistress!" Mlle. T. moved in quickly.

"No?" she asked, in feigned surprise. "Do you mean to say that you would not like to lie with these two beautiful girls, right

here upon this table, and make love to them?"

Allison seemed to be fighting to keep an expression of clear disgust from spreading over her face, still not certain of what her Mistress had in mind here. Was it some sort of test? What answer was she expecting to be given? The girl merely stammered for some moments without replying at all.

"I ask you again, Allison," Mlle. T. said, insistently. "Do you not want to lay these two beautiful young women upon this table, and make love with them, kiss them, lick them and suck them between their legs until they explode with delight all over...."

"Noooooooooooooo!" shrieked Allison, her shock at Mlle. T.'s words driving the cry of denial seemingly from the depths of the young girl's very soul. (Later evidence was to demonstrate that the actual feelings of that soul were in strong disagreement with this strong denial, as will be seen shortly.) Mlle. T. moved closer to the Allison's side, quickly soothing the girl in her obvious alarm and consternation.

"Very well, Allison," she said, calmly. "It's all right. We will have you do nothing at all that you do not wish to do. Your desires are what concern us here, and if you

do not wish to make love to other women, that is fine." Mlle. T. turned away from the girl to face me, catching my eye with an amused expression in her own, as she casually drew an object from somewhere about her person. It was a necklace, a long chain, of what appeared to be fine gold, from which dangled a single, glittering black stone, fully an inch across. This stone had been cut to display many facets, so that, as the stone hung there, gently turning, it sent out from its dark centre many hundreds of flashing sparkles of reflected light. It was arresting, a fascinating phenomenon to observe. Mlle. T. smiled, knowingly, at my reaction, and turned back toward the still-trembling Allison. The eyes of the young girl were instantly attracted to the glitter of the dark stone, just as mine had been, and the instant hers locked onto the sparkling gem, an unmistakable calm seemed to descend upon her, her breathing subsided somewhat, and some degree of her previous anxiety appeared to settle out. I watched as Mlle. T. slowly raised the dangling back stone to bring it closer before Allison's eyes. She leaned in to whisper some words to the girl that I was unable to decipher from where I stood. Allison's eyes became wide and

transfixed by the shining rays emitting from the dark jewel, as Mlle. T.'s whispered words continued. Then her eyes seemed to grow heavy, the lashes dropping gradually downward, ever downward, until Allison's eyes were closed completely. Mlle. T. now moved quietly back from the girl, who stood where the woman left her, seemingly asleep, or in some sort of trance. Mlle. T. returned now to my side, speaking to me.

"You are familiar with mesmerizm, Thomas?" she asked, quietly. I nodded. I had indeed heard of the strange work of M. Mesmer and his remarkable discovery. "I have learned the similar procedure you have just witnessed from Jo Lin," she continued. "As is usually the case, the oriental world has known of the process for many thousands of years. Our Allison is now under the influence of that procedure." I looked at the girl, standing motionless now, seemingly oblivious to what was happening around her. "The important aspect of the process, Thomas," continued Mlle. T., taking my arm and drawing me closer to the entranced young girl, " is that, while the doors unto Allison's subconscious mind are now open, and therefore Allison herself is now open to any suggestion we might make

to her, we can cause her to do nothing whatsoever that she would not ordinarily, in her nature, be inclined to do. We cannot force her to behave in any way that is inconsistent with her own inner nature. Do you see?" I did see. Mlle. T. went on to explain that all that had been pierced by the mesmerization process were Allison's outward defenses. The unnatural restraints, by which the young girl held her natural self in bondage, could now be temporarily overcome. Under her Mistress's suggestion now, Allison would behave just as she would naturally be inclined to do if it were not for those unnatural and, therefore, false and unhealthy, restraints that kept the girl thus enslaved, a slave to her own unhealthy inhibitions. Mlle. T. turned once gain to her subject, standing close by her ear to whisper low. "Now, Allison, my dear. Can you hear me?" The girl murmured indistinctly, as if in sleep. "Louder, Allison. We cannot hear you."

"Yes, Mistress." The voice was audible now, though still small.

"Allison," said Mlle. T. "I wish to ask you a question. But first, I want you to open your eyes." The girl did so, her eyes appearing to stare straight ahead without

seeing anything at all. "Do you see your two sisters, here?" asked Mlle. T., gesturing towards the two young blondes. Allison's eyes seemed to focus, now, her gaze directed at the two fair beauties across the room.

"Yes, Mistress," said the girl, without hesitation.

"Do you think they are beautiful, Allison?" the woman asked.

"Yes, Mistress," answered Allison, again without pause.

"Do you find them exciting to look upon?" Allison tilted her head to one side, as if considering the question.

"Yes," she decided, and said so succinctly. There was nothing whatsoever remaining of the girl's former reticence at such intimate questioning. As Mlle. T. had predicted, now that Allison's inhibitions had been magically removed through the miracle of mesmerizm, the girl's deepest, most private natural impressions and inclinations were now entirely open to our examination.

"Now, Allison," said Mlle. T., lowering her mouth to whisper more closely into the girl's ear. "I want to ask you another question." I sensed that a moment of crisis, or truth, had come, as I heard Mlle. T. whisper, "Would you like to make love to

these two, Allison? Would you like to hold them, and lick them, and cause them to spend into your adoring little mouth?"

Allison's breathing seemed to grow instantly deeper, more laboured, but it was not the excitation of fear and apprehension such remarks had instilled in the girl a moment or two earlier when her Mistress had posed her the very same question. No, this time Allison's small breast was rising and falling with an excitement she had denied herself until now, excitement at the thought of making love to one of her own sex. Again, the dark-haired girl's answer came instantly, though breathlessly, as I have said. "Yes," the girl whispered.

Mlle. T. smiled with evident satisfaction. "Then you shall, my dear. By all means, you shall." She motioned to the two naked blondes, who moved at their Mistress's bidding to seat themselves, side by side, upon the long edge of the oaken dining table before the three of us. Their knees parted without instruction, and I gazed, I must admit, somewhat lustily at closely trimmed fur of bright gold which crowned the summit of each girl's pink nether lips as they revealed them before us. Mlle. T. moved behind Allison, and pressed the girl

downward into a kneeling position before her two seated sisters.

Again, the Mistress spoke whisperingly into the young girl's ear. "Now, Allison, my dear. You know what to do. You can easily please another girl as you would go about pleasing yourself. The playful caresses you bestow upon your own pink loveliness each night beneath your bed sheets can be employed upon these, your sisters. You know what these sensations are, and you know how to achieve them. Simply follow your instincts and you cannot go astray."

Mlle. T. moved back from the kneeling girl, nodded to the seated young women, and then said, simply, "You may begin." Young Allison dove instantly forward between the parted thighs of the girl seated to her left, as quickly as if she had been propelled there! I saw her sweet young tongue dart from between her parted lips in the second before her open mouth plunged down upon the seated girl's pink vulva, engulfing the whole in an almost frantic, deep kiss! The blonde being so attended to arched her strong back, her spine actually creaking under the stretching strain of what the worshipping girl was causing her to feel.

"Ahhhhhhhhhh!" The seated girl sighed, her head thrown back, and a smile of delight spreading like sunshine over her exquisite face. Next to her, the second blonde gazed upon her sister's pleasure with calm approval, serene in the knowledge that her own pleasure would come soon enough. Audible slurping and sucking sounds came to us all from beneath Allison's bowed young face, her head turning slightly to the left or to the right with quick movements, like a small bear, burrowing for honey within the hollow mouth of a cone-laden tree, eager not to miss a single stray drop. It was not long before the ripe melons upon the chest of the young blonde began to heave with the approach of her crisis. Ecstatic gasps swelled into small, high, up-turning cries of joy, as the young woman reached her critical moment.

"Aghhhhhhhhhhhhhhh!" the golden-haired girl screamed out at last, as her young body began to shiver and quake in her tremendous orgasm. Allison obviously noted her first subject's time had for the moment passed, for now she shifted, knee-walking to the right in order to provide the same tender services for the second blonde-haired beauty, as the first sat absently petting her

well-attended slit, eyes closed in peaceful post-orgasmic bliss. The adoration of Allison's second conquest of the evening was completed even more quickly than the first. Obviously, the girl, while already having in her possession a precocious natural ability at such things - as, Mlle. T. assured me, all young females possess - she had developed even greater proficiency with the small degree of experience she was now accruing. The girl learned quickly, and there was even a hint of panic in the wild response of the second young blonde as Allison brought her home, kicking and screaming, into orgasm. There were even a few tears sparkling there in the wide, deep blue eyes, as the gratefully welcomed contractions went on and on, threatening, perhaps, never to stop.

The evening was far from over, for Mlle. T. instructed Allison once again into the sexual breech of the first seated young woman. And then, having delved deeply there and found yet another, stronger, orgasmic response, Allison returned to the second pretty pink mouth proffered, until, at length, the two fortunate young women had spent their pleasure upon the tongue of their younger sister a full dozen times, and lay

upon their backs along the table, exhausted and begging for a much-needed respite. And throughout all, the trance that still lay upon the dark-haired Allison remained unbroken, the girl unaware in her conscious mind of what long-withheld fantasies she was playing out here for her Mistress's observance, and my education, as well.

CHAPTER THIRTEEN - KAREN

I have now to describe briefly the strangest scene I was ever to witness during all my years at the Chateau Noir. For, indeed, this, my first visit to the black Chateau, was not to be my last. I have returned again and again to that dark estate throughout my life. But in all that time, in all the many midnight ceremonies and forbidden, secret rites and I attended, nothing was as strange or as wonderful as what I saw on the night that the fiery-haired Karen was to be trained.

Karen, you will recall, was the red-haired young woman of eighteen years, one of the girls I had been introduced to by Mlle. T. on my first night as her guest.

Mlle. T. had mentioned that in certain ancient civilizations there had developed the practice of utilizing adders in dark, religious rites concerned with the worship of sexual ecstasy. It was the sting of the adder that was so used. Mlle. T. had noted as well that Cleopatra, renowned queen of the Egyptian

Nile, was herself rumoured to have died while attempting the art. It was reputed to have been the bite of one of these snakes upon the nipple of one of her breasts that had stilled her heart at the peak of a poison induced state of erotic splendour.

But Mlle. T. had claimed upon the occasion of relating to me these supposed historical facts that she had found out the flaw that had proved fatal to that ancient queen. The solution to the problem of achieving this serpent induced ecstatic state was to prepare the subject with gradually increasing doses of the very poison that made the dark adder's sting for deadly. It was further revealed that, through many trials, it had been discovered by my host that women of the red-haired trait were, for some as yet unknown reason, more immune to these refined poisons, and so more likely to possess the strength and endurance to experience the exquisitely painful pleasure induced by the serpent's sting without succumbing to that sting's more deadly side-effect.

Karen, indeed, wore a crowning glory of hair as red as fire. And for some months previous, and totally unknown to herself, she had been consuming ever-increasing doses

of the deadly essence of those strange and exotic Egyptian Black Adder, imported at much expense to the Chateau and carefully distilled by the mysterious Jo Lin, who among her many other exotic talents, was a skilled medical chemist and herbalist, and had been working with the Chateau's Mistress for some time in effort to bring their experiment to the conclusion I was now about to witness.

I had not seen young Karen, she of the flaming tresses, emerald eyes, and strong, full breasts, since that first night when we had been introduced. I remembered how the young woman had screamed and struggled in unrestrained fear and horror at her fate when it had been revealed to her my her Mistress, and I recalled my last glimpse her as she was forcibly born from the room within the strong, confining arms of the servant Karl.

From that day until now, Karen had been kept bound and locked away within the Chateau's nether vaults, deep beneath the building's stone foundations, a portion of the Chateau to which I, as yet, had never been invited.

But I instantly recognized the young woman I now saw as that same Karen, and

the same wild look of insane panic screamed out from the face that I now saw, mouth rubber-bitted and tightly gagged, and bandaged from upper lip to chin.

The girl hung in the small room into which I had just been led, suspended upright in the air from four long lengths of heavy chain, one shackled to each of the girl's extremities. It seemed that no bindings of simple leather were to be trusted with restraining the young woman through the fantastic ordeal she was about to endure. Her chained, naked body formed a human "X", arms stretched high and apart by the two spans of chain running upwards and outward to a system of pulleys fixed to large, wooden beams at the chamber's ceiling. Identical sections of linked iron stretched outward and downward to where they were padlocked to iron rings set into the chamber's stone floor.

Once fixed, and the upper stretches tightened through the workings of the heavy pulleys, young Karen was drawn into the aforementioned "X" figure as tightly and unyieldingly as a bowstring about to snap.

The red-haired beauty was entirely naked, her large, full breasts and sweetly open nether mouth were vulnerable to

whatever the Chateau's Mistress might desire. She hung with tears of panic and dread already coursing down her cheeks to drip wetly from her fear-erected nipples.

I will make quick work of describing the singular rite which was now performed with out dwelling upon the indelicate details. Suffice it to say that the dark Jo Lin entered the chamber, accompanied by two younger Orientals, who I later learned were apprentices to this mistress of many unusual talents.

Each woman carried, carefully cradled in her arms, a small, earthen-wear jar with many strange etchings in some uncertain language upon it's curved outer surface and capped with a heavy-looking lid of the same earthen material. These three jars, I guessed, must each contain the small serpents that were to serve as triggers for the Mistress's experiment.

Now, as Mlle. T. had described in those mystic rites of old, the three women approached their subject and, as one, quickly unsealed the wide mouths of their three jars and pressed them into their prescribed places upon the body of young Karen. Jo Lin's two apprentices held the mouths of their two jars so that the circling mouths encompassed the

girl's twin, red nipples. And the oriental beauty herself pressed the opening of the remaining jar into the junction of the girl's straining young thighs.

All three held the vessels tightly in place, while all in the room, myself, Mlle. T. and both her servants, Karl and Alex looked silently on. There was a hush throughout the chamber, as all eyes focused on the naked form of the red-haired girl hanging suspended before us.

Karen, herself, looked wildly around at us all, beseeching us in an unspoken plea to show her some mercy. Then the young woman's eyes darted down to the jar at her left breast. She wriggled at some odd sensation that was undoubtedly centred at the flesh beneath the earthenware mouth. Then her eyes grew huge, and a loud, unearthly scream erupted from beneath her gag and muffler.

It was known instinctively by all that the first of the three serpents, that one within the jar at Karen's left breast, had found the sweet pap of the girl's erect and tempting nipple, and had bit home.

Scream followed scream, as the girl wriggled an bucked the little she could within her bonds, her face red with the

exquisite pain that was shooting out from her molested breast to radiate through her entire body. Then her eyes shifted abruptly to her right, her torso whipping instinctively in the opposite direction, and another, stronger scream of horror exploded from her obstructed throat. The serpent at her right breast had struck.

The body of the young woman whipped and shimmied about, though her movements were restricted to those such as a plucked harp string might be capable of, as her already overloaded system fought to accept and somehow deal with this new intensity of searing, torturous, discomfort.

Then, even in her excruciating pain, a realization seemed to come to her, and she froze in her unavailing struggles to concentrate all her attention to the jar that Jo Lin stiff held immovable at the junction of the girl's tautly opened thighs. Karen had suddenly realized that this third jar, placed so suggestively at the very centre of her vulnerable femininity, must certainly contain the coiled form of a serpent as well.

She seemed to attempt to pull herself heavenward with all her womanly strength in a frantic, though futile, effort to escape the inevitable. Then her entire body froze in

a ridged spasm of unendurable agony, her emerald eyes rolled upward until only their snowy whites showed, and Karen let forth a sudden scream that would have rivaled the cry of a dying banshee. Dogs throughout the countryside would have no doubt echoed her cry as coming from one of their own in dire torment, had the chamber not been heavily soundproofed and so hidden from all ears beyond, human, animal or otherwise.

The unearthly cries followed one after the other, for many long minutes, and perhaps the angels heard poor Karen's cry, or possibly those long-sleeping gods and goddesses of Old Egypt, so a gradual change seemed to come over young Karen. The terrible, racking torment of the triple adder stings began having their secondary, and more desirous effects upon the subject of Mlle. T.'s experiment.

The Mistress herself seemed to note this before the rest of us, for she now moved forward to more closely examine her young subject. Karen's head was lolling slowly from side to side, though her green eyes remained as wide as ever.

Mlle. T. motioned for Jo Lin and her two attending apprentices to remove the serpent jars. The three did so, pulling the open

mouths of the their jars away and quickly resealing them with their heavy lids before the small creatures could make good any escape. When Jo Lin pulled the open mouth of the jar covering Karen's sex, it was found that the serpent within had remained attached to the girl where it had chosen to bite her. It now hang, all thirteen inches of it, from the small pink morsel of Karen's young clitoris.

Even the two apprentices gasped at the sight of this, and the ever calm Jo Lin gave them each look that clearly communicated her extreme displeasure at their squeamish reaction. The two girls were immediately cowed, and I wondered what dread form of chastisement would certainly await these two later on.

Jo Lin's careful hands skillfully caught up the dangling serpent, a delicately manicured thumb and forefinger catching the creature just behind it's clenching jaws. The adder involuntarily released its hold on the clit of the red-haired girl, and the older woman returned the thing to its jar, capping the mouth with the fitted lid, and drawing away from the suspended figure, along with her two assistants.

Mlle. T., however, took no note at all of these happenings. Her attention was fixed the changed state of the young woman who hung chained before us. The bitten flesh at Karen's nipples glowed a hot red against the pale softness that surrounded it, and the small bud of the poor girl's adder bitten clit had swollen and extended itself redly nearly half an inch in length above the wetly divided lips below.

But Mlle. T. was watching the young woman's eyes. The wildness there appeared to be rapidly fading, replaced by a vague expression, almost of wonder or surprise.

"It is happening," Mlle. T. murmured, as she continued to observe her experiment closely. "Soon, now... very soon," she said, her voice quiet, but tinged with an excitement I had not heard her emote at any time previous.

It was just then that Karen gave a surprised little gasp from beneath her gag. Her body stiffened, as it had done before when each of the three stinging serpents had driven home their twin fangs, but this time, instead of a cry at some unimaginably tormenting pain, the stiffening of Karen's body preceded what appeared to be a small shiver of pleasure. The young woman

actually gurgled in delight, as the rippling shiver passed through her naked frame, leaving a field of tiny goose flesh across the pale skin in its wake.

A small laugh was heard, and there was a clear expression of joy in Karen's eyes, which was suddenly shattered by a look of renewed panic as another, even stronger ripple of pleasure shivered through the girl's strong frame. Soon Karen's body was convulsing almost constantly in what had the appearance of one, long, extended orgasm.

Mlle. T. was smiling and nodding her head quietly, as if this is what she had hoped for and expected.

In a few moments, Karen was bucking and writhing against her chains as insistently as she had earlier under the painful triple sting of the adders, but now her shrieks, as high, long and heart-rending as those she had emitted previously, were not cries of pain but those of the most intense pleasure.

Again and again, the girl rose, strained, and screamed her pleasure to the heavens. Sometimes a trembling, shivering, gurgling laugh would separate one long cry from the next, as if the girl could not restrain her wonder and delight at the pleasures she was now experiencing.

"H... how...?" My dry throat nearly choked off my question. "How long will it last?" I finally managed to ask.

Mlle. T., her eyes still upon the orgasming girl, shrugged. "No one can tell," she said. "A young woman of Karen's youth and virility... she should last longer than her sisters who have gone before. If her heart can hold up without bursting, we will at last know how long the pleasurable symptoms can last. That would be most desirable."

I wondered for a moment about all those "sisters who have gone before." I considered asking as the details of their fate, but thought better of it.

The detailed results of the Mlle. T.'s experiment with Karen will wait for another time. It is a long story in itself, and I must move on now to bring my own story to a conclusion.

The rest can wait.

CHAPTER FOURTEEN - INITIATION

It was some few days later that I came to know the larger purpose for my presence at the Chateau Noir. I had dined early one evening with Mlle. T., not in the great dining room as was our custom, but in the small sitting room adjoining her own bed chamber.

When the plates had been cleared from the small table by the ever-silent Karl, Mlle. T. sat me on a leather upholstered sofa, offered me a small neat brandy, and stood facing me.

"Thomas," she said. "There is an important part of our training regimen here at the Chateau that I have not yet mentioned to you. You are aware that our purpose and goal is to raise up the finest courtesans in the world."

Mlle. T. turned to pace slowly back and forth before me, as she continued. "Our girls, once they have left these premises, will know all there is to know about pleasing a man. They must be experts, therefore, not

only in receiving pleasure from a man, but in offering pleasure as well."

The Mistress of the Chateau Noir stopped her pacing, and stood facing me once more. "You have seen some of the many methods we employ here to teach our girls to enjoy the pleasures of the flesh, but we have said little about how we instruct our students in giving as good as they get."

Mlle. T. paused a moment for effect, then said, "And that is why you are here, Thomas."

My mouth fell open, not comprehending what the Mistress was saying. "You, Thomas, were sent here to my school for two purposes. One, your uncle wished you to have some knowledge of the world as your full adulthood approaches, and so you were sent to me to see what you have so far seen. You will see and know much more, if you consent to fulfill the second purpose for your presence here."

I sat, the fine brandy in my hand forgotten, as I waited to learn what this second purpose might be.

"The girls," said Mlle. T., finally, "at a certain stage in their training, need first-hand experience of the male sex."

A glimmer of what Mlle. T. might be implying sparkled at the edge of my mind. "First-hand... physical... experience," added the Mistress, making her purpose clear at last.

"There is simply no substitute for it," she continued. "And, while Karl and Alex certainly have the qualifications to do what is necessary, they would find it all quite too exhausting to fulfill such duties and attend to the requirements of their regular jobs here. The male chosen must, I feel, be someone younger, whose youthful energies can be dedicated solely to these specialized activities in the training of my girls. Someone like you, Thomas."

Mlle. T. sat by side now on the dark leather of the sofa. She spoke seductively in my ear, so that I flushed warmly at each of her words. "Think of it, Thomas!" she whispered, intently. "You will go back into the world as knowledgeable in the ways of love as any man alive. There will be no female anywhere in the world that you will not know how to win. The choice will yours, for all women will fall at your feet, demanding the love that in all their lives only you will know how to give."

Mlle. T. looked upon my stunned countenance for a long moment. "Do not answer as yet, my dear boy," she said. "I have promised your esteemed uncle that I would expose you to at least a few of the experiences a young man should have before entering the world. It is the least I owe him for the many years of support he has given our school."

Before I could offer any protest or comment, Mlle. T. clapped her hands three times, sharply, and there entered into the room three of the Chateau's older students, these being a blonde, a brunette, and a red-head, each appearing to be of about nineteen-years of age. All three were dressed the usual short tunic of wispy white silk.

"These students are to be your instructors, my dear Thomas," said Mlle. T. "Daphne, Rebecca, and Sabrina," she added, by was of brief introduction. As each of their names were called, the girls shrugged out of their tunics, and revealed themselves in all their glorious nudity. All three had hair cut into short pageboy styles, and the colour of each was accented by the brief shadow of matching colour between their long legs.

Daphne and Rebecca, the blonde and the brunette, respectively, approached my person without the slightest hesitancy, and perfunctorily began unbuttoning my waistcoat and shirt. The red-headed Sabrina went to work at the buttons of my pants. I had not the opportunity to ever consider escape, but was in the very next moment entirely as naked as my instructresses.

My member was hugely erect before me, as the three young women pulled me toward the Mistresses bedroom. I was somewhat alarmed that the three obviously intended me to invade the sanctity of their Mistress's bed for what was to follow, but one despairing look toward the Mademoiselle herself assured me as to her willing consent to this intrusion. Swirling her brandy absently in the large glass snifter, she moved unconcernedly to follow the four of us into the other room.

The girls and I fell upon the bed as one, and instantly I felt the delicious sensation on a warm, welcoming mouth enveloping the straining length of my ridged member. I felt as if I might explode, so intense was the intimate caress, one, of course, that I had never before experienced. The other two nymphs began to offer kisses all along the

rest of my quickly overheating body. Their lips touched and sucked at me everywhere, first up around my neck and then down across my heaving chest to my stomach. Once, the lips of both came to rest momentarily upon that tight, wrinkled sack beneath the ever-straining shaft that plunged so affably within their sister's mouth above. My fingers lightly caressed the blonde hair of that sweet worshipper, as I felt my trembling young balls sucked into the mouth of first one, then the other of her two accomplices.

Suddenly, I knew my moment of crisis was approaching, that I was about to spend my startled passion into the mouth that was servicing me there. But at once the blonde seemed to recognize the moment as well, and she pulled away before the final rush had been triggered. My poor lance twitched and throbbed in disappointment, but exulted anew as the girl swung above me to plunge the wet sheath of her warm sex fully down upon the rod her young mouth had adored but a moment before.

If what I had felt before was a wonder, then what I was experiencing now was a true miracle! Nothing I had known in my brief life had thrilled me to this amazing extent.

My heart, my mind, my very soul echoed the cries of exquisite pleasure that now coursed throughout my person. I felt that I might die here and now, and be glad of it, passing into the next life fully satisfied that I had known the absolute best that this earthly life had to offer.

Again, the moment of my pleasure began to arrive, and this time there was no attempt to delay its completion. Indeed, when the knowledgeable young blonde recognized my approaching climax, she doubled the already rapid speed of her riding, and it was she that first achieved the state of orgasm, writhing up high upon my passion tortured shaft to come crashing down again with high scream of delight. This cry triggered my own, and I felt a fiery bursting within my straining loins that radiated throughout my entire person, finally exploding in a huge, gushing rush of sperm from my resounding balls up through the length of my granite-hard prick, filling the sweet cavity of the young blonde with juices of my own to mix with her squirted spendings from within.

Before I came to myself, before the stars that obscured my vision had dispersed, I felt myself being shifted over onto my side and then over further, onto the top of one of the

other girls. I opened my eyes to find myself face to face with the deep, brown, knowing eyes of the Rebecca, the brunette, her arms embracing me tightly, as I felt other feminine hands guiding my still ridged cock into the soft, warmly engulfing, wet sex of the girl, in the second manly conquest of my young life.

This ecstatic ride was at a slower pace than the one that had proceeded it. The loving hips of the young girl churned and writhed with a deliberate, measured insistence beneath me, while I instinctively matched pace with slow, deeply rooting plunges from above. I have no idea how long our pleasure simmered along below boiling point, but eventually I felt again the ageless rise of urgency signaling a quickly approaching eruption. The knowing young woman seemed to sense as much, just as her sister had done a few moments before, and the churning of her hips became a demanding series of fast, sharp, staccato hunchings, clearly designed to pull from me that which I was willingly about to give.

The two of us exploded and crashed together, my vision once more becoming a bright universe of flashing stars, as I collapsed in exquisite bliss.

Once more, I was pulled up from my repose. Rebecca and Daphne, the two thieves of my previous virginity, held me from each side, guiding me onto my knees before what I now saw was the kneeing form of Sabrina, the fiery red-head. She faced away from me, and looked at me over her shoulder. It was the rear of this girl that was now offered me, I now understood. But understanding was unnecessary. The slender fingers of Sabrina's companions did the work of guiding my, as yet, somehow unreduced erectness to its nest intended target.

For a moment, however, I suspected their aim to less than true, for I looked down to find the tip of my young cock nudging, not the red curl-fringed gate of the girl's sex, but the narrower opening above. My hips braced, lest I be prodded from behind into entering that forbidden channel before my two attendants noticed their mistake.

But there was no mistake. I saw the hand of the owner of that dark passage, herself, reach from below her divided rear to spread apart the cheeks there, and so make my entrance all the easier. Before the shock of the realization had passed, the two girl pushed me from behind, and the long, hard

shaft of my manhood was plunged in a single thrust to depths of the third young woman's waiting bottom.

The red-head threw back her head and screamed, though with pain of pleasure I knew not. I suspect now that it was in response to a combination of both. Encouraged by the urging hands of the girls now at my side, I entered into a fast, almost violent thrusting and plunging, the kneeling redhead pushing back eagerly to meet me with each long stroke. It was mere seconds before, for the third time within the hour, I felt my gushing essence come rushing up and out into a welcoming female orifice.

I was a virgin no longer. All promises from Mlle. T. to my uncle had been satisfied, and now it was up to me as to whether I would leave the Chateau Noir now and take my newly acquired knowledge out into the world, or whether I would remain, and experience far more than I could now even guess.

I made my decision even as I knelt there upon the bed, my face cradled along the sleek, sweat-dampened back of the red-haired young woman I had just conquered, and I communicated my answer to Mlle. T. with a single silent look.

The Mistress of the Chateau Noir smiled her approval.

CHAPTER FIFTEEN - INTO SERVICE

There began at this point some weeks of training for me at the Chateau Noir. Mlle. T. informed succinctly me that before I could be employed in the preparation of her young students I must come to know much more about eliciting the pleasuring of the female than what I had discovered so far. I will skip past most of this period until, perhaps, another time, and will relate instead an event which occurred when my training was finally complete.

One morning I was called to report once again to Mlle. T.'s bed chamber. As I entered, I saw young Allison, the seventeen-year-old beauty that I had seen undergoing the Mistress's mesmerization treatment many weeks before, and had seen nothing whatsoever of since.

The girl had been strapped, face downward, along a narrow, leather upholstered ottoman, about seven inches

wide and four or five feet in length, supported at each end by two equally padded legs forming a wide inverted "V". The dark-haired girl had been positioned with her belly along the top of this ottoman, with her legs tightly strapped to the wide-spread legs at one end, so that her two rear entrances were readily exposed and vulnerable to whatever attentions, or intrusions, her Mistress might desire. The young woman's arms had been stretched tightly forward along the ottoman by leather straps fixing her wrists together to the ottoman's far end, leaving her with very little mobility above her waist and none at all below it.

The girl was not bitted or gagged, and it was clear from the frightened way in which she stretched her head to see what we did behind her that the girl was not on this occasion under the calming effects of mesmerizm

Besides young Allison, only Mlle. T. awaited me there in the small room, and without prelude she explained my purpose for being there.

"You remember our Allison, don't you, Thomas?" asked Mlle. T. I nodded silently in response, as I had been taught. Whatever part I might take in any proceedings

regarding a girl's training at the Chateau, I had been cautioned that only Mlle. T. was to speak aloud. So I awaited Mlle. T.'s pleasure without comment.

"You have seen young Allison at play with some of her fellow students," reminded the Mistress. I did, indeed, remember how the nervous, dark-haired girl strapped prone before me had licked and tongue-tickled the two blonde playmates into dozens of orgasms while in the mesmerizing spell of Mlle. T.'s black pendant.

The girl, herself, knew of the event her Mistress was speaking about. She blushed furiously in acute embarrassment at the very mention of it, her entire body reddening all the way into the sweet divide of her widely parted buttocks.

"You have seen our Allison at play while under the effects of mesmerizm, but since that time, Thomas, I have observed her enjoying those same games, but without the influence of M. Mesmer's process. Young Allison has become quite the young slut where her sister students are concerned. Once the floodgates of her secret, natural passions were opened, the girl you see before you has embraced those lascivious

delights with as much enthusiasm as I have ever noted in a student."

The girl being so intimately discussed wriggled uncomfortably upon the ottoman, her motion causing a small creaking sound of leather against leather, as she attempted in vain to shift her position.

"But now, my dear Thomas, the time has come to for our Allison to move forward into new frontier, a move which she has adamantly resisted for some time."

Here Allison gave a small start, as if knowing what "new frontier" her Mistress was referring to, and demonstrating exactly the reluctance the older woman had indicated. She twisted and writhed against her bonds. But all held fast.

"I will ask you again, Allison. Will you now willingly submit to the initiation into the frontier you have for so long avoided? I promise you the pleasures are even greater than those you have experienced so far."

The response of the girl was very clear. "Noooooooooooo!" she screamed, in defiance. I knew this to be a mistake upon her part, and was surprised that the girl did not seem to know it herself.

"Very well," said Mlle. T., amicably enough. "If that is what you wish, so be it.

It is most certainly your decision to make, and I will faithfully abide by it."

Allison dropped her head forward in obvious relief. But her face rocketed abruptly upward in the very next instant, as Mlle. T. brought the length of a long, thin, black buggy whip down across the young girls widely parted rear cheeks in a quick, single stroke with the sharp, cracking report of a pistol shot. The whip had apparently been secreted somewhere beneath the ottoman, and Mlle. T. had retrieved it without having been seen doing so by Allison, so that the smacking stroke across her delicate behind was completely unexpected.

"Aghhhhhhhhhhh!" Allison screamed in horrible pain, her entire frame bucking and tossing upon the ottoman, the tight straps of her binding stretching even more taught than they had before. Nearly a dozen equally forceful strokes from the thin whip quickly followed the first. The howling, straining young woman was given no quarter whatsoever. There was scarcely sufficient tome to catch her breath at the end of each long scream of torment. At the end, the girl was babbling incoherently, and it was apparently to hear the content of this pain-

garbled communication that Mlle. T. finally paused in the whipping.

For some moments, Allison appeared now incapable of speech. She continued to screech and gasp as the pain of those last, final strokes continued to reverberate through her system. Long, thin lines of deepest red in a criss-crossing mass if whip-brands covered the girl's sweet behind from its lower curve all the way to the base of her spine.

The frantic writhing under the crashing whip had made one other alteration in the appearance of the girl's young rear. The plump, pink lips of Allison's small sex had been separated by the wild motion of her hips, until now the doorway to that honeyed channel was invitingly open before our view.

"You wish to say something, Allison?" asked Mlle. T., somewhat mockingly. "Perhaps you wish now to give your consent to my wishes?"

"I... I... Oh!" the girl still could not quite find her tongue, though she clearly struggled to do so. Her eyes were frantic and wide, though perhaps unseeing. "I... I..."

"I see," said Mlle. T., calmly, and without preamble began suddenly again with the whip. Allison's shrill, surprised shrieks

were almost deafening this time, as again she writhed and bucked under a fast, fierce whipping from behind.

A dozen or so strokes later, Mlle. T. paused once again, but the girl strapped before her continued to wail and caterwaul as if the whipping was still in progress. Her discomfort at this point must have been extreme.

"Now," said Mlle. T., somewhat breathless now from the effort of swinging the long whip in such a number of rapid strokes. "Is there something you wish to say to me, Allison?"

The girl drew a single, convulsive intake breath... and screamed out her answer. "Yesssssssssssssssss!"

"Might you wish to say that you will willingly submit to what I desire, what you, yourself, desire, if you were but honest with your own self? Might that be what you wish to say, Allison?"

Allison once again drew a long breath, and shrieked her assent.

"Very well, then," said Mlle. T., as if expecting the girl's agreement all along, not having doubted it for an instant.

"Thomas," said Mlle. T., as she put aside her whip and motioned me forward.

"Thomas, Allison here is no virgin where her sister females are concerned, but she remains so where the opposite sex is concerned. I wish you to remedy that situation, Thomas, and I wish you to do so now."

I looked at Mlle. T., and then at the girl bound before me, paused but an instant, and then preparing my self to obey.

I was stripped below the waist an instant later, and now stood before the proffered, whip-marked cheeks of young Allison, prepared to forcibly remove the virginity that remained deep within her. Mlle. T.'s instruction of the past weeks had been thorough on this subject, and I knew well the careful techniques that would make the experience as pleasant as possible for a young woman being mounted for the very first time.

First I knelt down behind the girl, and examined the parted pink lips that stood sentry at the gates though which I was about to plunge into the sweet virgin channel beyond. The lips were full, but delicate, and a simple caressing and stroking of these tender tissues was soon rewarded my a honey-scented flow of moisture from between them.

The girl's hips were trembling now, as her in-born feminine nature began to take hold, as Mlle. T. had assured me it would, and the small thrills of arousal began to raise goose flesh along her whip-reddened buttocks, and upward along her smooth back as well. She began to murmur to herself indistinctly now as well, the small sounds she uttered nearly too low to detect.

I now added the caresses of my lips, by this time well practiced upon the intimate flesh of dozens of the Chateau's students, to those of my fingers, and felt a deep shiver erupt throughout the body of the bound young woman. I had to this point avoided the pleasure point of Allison's little pink clitoris, saving such direct stimulation for the critical that was fast approaching. The little bud trembled and vibrated just above my lips, eagerly stretching forth it's sweet head, as if actively seeking out such direct attentions.

I decided then that the moment had arrived, and took that sweet bud of erect flesh between my lips and sucked in suddenly as far into my mouth as it could be drawn.

Allison gasped, as if she had been touched there with flame or with ice, and

called out to the heavens in a wordless announcement of impending orgasm. Her cry shifted up an octave or two, as I added the flicking of my tongue against the little node to the sucking caress of my pursed lips.

Then the force of Allison's crisis exploded upon her in full, and for nearly a full minute she writhed and bucked and tossed against her leather bonds, and screamed and screamed and screamed.

Before the girl had time to recover, I stood up behind her, my lust-enraged manhood perfectly aligned with the opening of Allison's young sex, looked to Mlle. T. for her approval and permission, obtained both in a brief nod, and then plunged forcibly home.

The girl went insane against my pressing loins. Her shrieks grew higher and higher until they were beyond the capacity of men's ears to hear them. Hunting dogs for miles around would have been tortured my those cries, were it not for the soundproof corking in Chateau's thick walls.

Suffice it to say that when I finally withdrew my spent member, Allison was no longer the untouched virgin she had been moments before, and I am happy to note that the tears she shed after were heartfelt tears of

gratitude. Indeed, it was at the girl's insistence herself that she remain in her bonds until I had once again plunged my re-awakened manhood into her sweet orifice for another, longer session.

That night young Allison slept with me in my own chamber, and in my own bed, blissfully enjoying the newly discovered pleasures of male-female eroticism.

My period of active participation in the instruction and training of the future courtesans of the great Chateau Noir had begun.

AFTERWORD

I wish to add here a note or two about the underlying nature of Mlle. T.'s great theory regarding the proper training of young courtesans, as that nature has been revealed to me over my many visits to the Chateau Noir, both in my youth - the time of the narrative I have penned here - and in my middle years, now long gone as well.

The scholars of ancient Greece, among others, have noted that it is the female, and not the male, that holds the true secrets of Nature. For all of man's thrusting and parrying about in the world, it is always the female that finally, ultimately rules, for without Woman, mere Man is nothing!

Mlle. T. taught her students that the female, even when held in bondage to the male, must assuredly become the Mistress of her master. So, by perfectly aligning her girls toward the ultimate pleasuring of the male, she made those girls mistresses, both of themselves and of any man who might one day contract for their services.

There are many men, many great men, throughout the world, both in the East and in the West, who have been ruled by the girls of the Chateau Noir, and yet have remained blissfully unaware.

They, and I believe, the world have, on the whole, been much better for it.

- The End -

Made in the USA
Monee, IL
15 February 2022

91256891R00135